TEXT ME FROM
MANHATTAN

MAURICE P. FORTUNE

Author of Now Eye See and Living on Powdered Sugar

TEXT ME FROM MANHATTAN

iUniverse books may be ordered through booksellers or by contacting:

iUniverse
1663 Liberty Drive
Bloomington, IN 47403
www.iuniverse.com
1-800-Authors (1-800-288-4677)

Because of the dynamic nature of the Internet, any web addresses or links contained in this book may have changed since publication and may no longer be valid. The views expressed in this work are solely those of the author and do not necessarily reflect the views of the publisher, and the publisher hereby disclaims any responsibility for them.

Any people depicted in stock imagery provided by Getty Images are models, and such images are being used for illustrative purposes only. Certain stock imagery © Getty Images.

ISBN: 978-1-5320-8333-4 (sc)
ISBN: 978-1-5320-8332-7 (e)

Print information available on the last page.

iUniverse rev. date: 10/24/2019

TABLE OF CONTENTS

AUTHOR'S NOTE:

Somewhere between my obsession with African and African-American History, British Mysteries, countless biographies, salted and peppered with an occasional piece of science fiction, lay my sundered passion for short stories of life. I know that everyone who has lived for more than a few moments has a ton of short stories to tell. Realistically speaking, mine may or may not be anything special, Still, propelled by my emotions and compelled by need to put pen to paper I have set in motion this group of six writings. They are not presented because of my need for profit, I can think of several easier ways to make money. The stories are set to paper because, although presented as fiction, each is based upon a true- life person or persons and each has a story behind the story: a double entendre if you will. But they are fun stories as well. Someone once wrote that life mustn't be taken too seriously and I am a firm believer of that thought. So here they are, my third publication and I fervently hope not my last. I've broken all the rules and I'm sorry for that little piece of news but then, it's my book! I also hope you will read and enjoy them just. And if you find among them a word or phrase that rings home I hope you will remember that your story is just a pen stroke or a keypad away. Happy reading! - Maurice P. Fortune

TEXT ME FROM MANHATTAN
By Maurice P. Fortune

Text Me from Manhattan; if you've got the time.
Text a little secret and a crazy rhyme.
Tell me 'bout the crazies you saw riding on the rails.
Add a little humor 'bout the homeless; plus details!
I'll know what you're saying if you take time to describe
How you felt just standing in the queue to pay your ride.
Text the piece you mentioned of the argument you had
With that person who was nasty and the one who's just plain mad!
Of the pocketbooks and backpacks that were planted on the seats.
Text me of the fashions you see strolling in the streets.
Yes, text me from Manhattan if you're still my friend; my boo.
I can't make it all go viral but I'll text right back at you!

ALL CAME TUMBLING - (TOUT EST TOMBE)

"GIVE ME YOUR tired, your poor, your huddled masses yearning to breathe free!"- From "The New Colossus by Emma Lazarus -1875.

For a long minute I stood beneath the canopy of the bakery. It was comforting smelling the aroma of the sweet rolls and coffee as they wafted through the door. It soiled the air around me and engulfed the otherwise sour smell of the street trenches for nearly the entire length of the block. I didn't move. Equally transfixed by the sounds coming at me from the bakery's next door neighbor. I knew I was being held captive. But unlike the sweetness of the breads and rolls falling upon my nose, I was being imprisoned by sound: sounds that soothed my ears and stirred my inner soul. These were sounds that for a brief moment returned me to my roots in rural Maryland and maybe farther back to an ancestral home far, far away on the other side of the Atlantic. A place I would never know.

This was the sound of music and almost instinctively I hummed the melody in my head and decided that I was listening to a progression from the D major scale. It was a simple progression above a two-four rhythm and I'd played it by rote so many, many times that I'd lost count. One, six, two, five, one. Repeated over and over again, it was punctuated by hand clapping that kept time with foot stomping and an occasional shout or moan. I knew the rhythm and even though I could not get a visual picture of the scene I knew that too. After all I had grown up near those dirt roads that led to the small house of worship where I was a regular Sunday morning witness and participant in scenes very similar. The sounds were not alien to me.

But what made it somewhat different to me was the passion of the players. They were clearly "into" the music. It was alive and they were but messengers. It was different because of the feel of the music. A feeling that was distinctly un-American. The music bespoke a darkness and a freedom that can only be gained under the cover of night and perhaps to a people who had never before been subjugated by money or by power.

The keyboardist was supported by a lone electric bass player who thumped out a magical sound that I was sure had its origins in the African bush. There were voices above the music but they seemed almost superfluous. Maybe this was because I could not understand the language being sung. This was the place of the leaning gate. It was a place I had passed countless times since my arrival in the neighborhood. A group of stores and turn of the century dwellings perched on a main thoroughfare in Staten Island, New York.

I had stood in the bus stop just across the street or a few doors away. I had hovered beneath the tiny canopies of the stores to protect myself from the elements as I waited for the S46, S48 or the S62 to take me the short distance to the ferry terminal. I had waited and watched like all others as bus after bus rolled by ignoring our vigil even though they were bound for the same destination: the S91, S92, and the S96. After work I'd return home using the same route.

In fact, on this day I had just exited the bus preparing to walk the sixty-five paces to my doorstep. A Sunday afternoon in July, I had taken a leisurely stroll to the ferry terminal. There is a seafood restaurant there for tourists and I go there sometimes to sit alone looking out over the water, as I treat myself to a plate of fresh lobster. Returning to my abode I had never heard a sound coming from the small church. It was the church I'd dubbed, "l' eglise de la porte panchee," the church of the leaning gate! Walking fast one might miss the fact that it is a church but I had left used and sometimes almost new clothes and shoes on the doorstep. One could do that practically without being noticed: just walk up the four or five steps and leave your donation at the door.

It is also a place where, once a week, neighborhood folks stand in queue to grab bags of foodstuffs. Locally, the church is known for its distribution of free bags of milk, juices, and veggies. Can goods and even a turkey might sometimes be had here. I have never found it necessary to partake of the giveaways but I have watched as the lines fill up. They move quickly to allow space for yet one more needy and sometimes greedy taker to load arms or shopping carts with their share of the freebies. Even late in the evening of the giveaways and when the crowds have disappeared, a hungry soul might yet be rewarded with several cans of the left-over goods. They can be found neatly lined up just for the taking, on the concrete ledge of the trash area of the sanctuary.

In a sense, the church mirrors the neighborhood. This is a mostly immigrant section and it is transient too. Aside from the ever-changing signs announcing one more closing and another opening or "under new management" are the faces of the populace. One can see in the faces of the people the telltale signs and expressions of the places they came from. There are the strong features of the aborigines of Mexico.

The striking and dark faces of Africa stand out alongside an occasional head of blonde tresses and very pale skin: the badge of distinction worn by some Eastern Europeans. One can also find here the young and exuberant expressions of my own people: the Black Americans. This year they've adopted a new way to express themselves. Their "new" way is simply one that's been warmed over and borrowed several times from the past. It is a throw-back to something my people have used and thrown aside at least 4 times in my memory. It's a "Doo-Rag" and I've seen them all before but it has been slightly elongated and more colors have been added. Somehow, with the extra material hanging from the back of the rag it looks conspicuously like something that should be saved for a desert people. Maybe the Taureg peoples of the Sahara Desert could make a more efficient use of the thing. And not to be outdone, some of our females have saved the best for last. They have decided that their hair should hang very long. It must be flowing and hang down the back like wings of a Flamingo or maybe a Condor. The hair must be colored blue or red and sometimes pink and orange. It looks odd to say the least. Especially on the old but I am comforted just knowing that the styles will not last, They will be discarded and go the way of the torn and tattered jeans, just as the 4-5 inch heels and the skirts and dresses they were almost wearing just 2 short seasons ago.

But in the midst of this, almost in stark contrast, one comes face face-to-face with the masks of desperation and hopelessness. Walking the short block it is not difficult to be asked more than once for pocket change: money to buy food or a cup of coffee. Even seventy-five cents to subsidize the drinking habits of some poor soul who is down on his luck is politely requested. Very often some brazen female will approach to offer sexual favors in return for just a few dollars or a night's sleep,

But this story has another place of origin and it begins long before one meets the saga of despair that lies in the streets and on a clear day, sits on the stoops of this boulevard in Staten Island. It is a tale that begins miles away and across the waters of the bay and it lies in the mean streets and tunnels of the main island. In many ways Staten Island is the end of the story rather than the beginning. Staten Island is the fifth rather than the first and somehow, in my mind it makes the whole bushel of apples even more rotten. It points out even more poignantly the nastiness and the divide between the haves and the have nots in this place lovingly termed, "the Big Apple" but is very often referred to as the rotten apple. The place I too have fallen in love with but cannot help but dub a place where, all can come TUMBLING DOWN.

LEAVING MANHATTAN

The Select bus pulls up to the curb and I climb aboard and grab a seat. Even though the hour is relatively late for homebound riders like me there are few seats available. I sit alone until the bus stops at Second Avenue. A short man with a huge backpack strapped to him sits next to me. It brings a smile to my face when I realize he has turned his back to me, ignoring the fact that the thing is almost planted in my lap. But he begins texting just like most of the other riders. There are about twenty passengers and many of them are texting. Others are wearing earphones and they all seem unaware that they will need to get off the bus in just a few blocks.

It had been a busy day at work and I'd left a bit late. It was just before seven by the time the Select Bus deposited me at 34th and Broadway and just in front of the side door of the iconic giant that is known as Macy's Department Store. I ignored the temptation to go in to browse the section of men's shirts. It was the last thing I needed- another eighty dollars shirt by some Italian or American designer whose shops, in two or three months, would find another way to rip us off by changing the shape of the shirt collar or by making the shirt a bit tighter or loose. I would fall for it again just like I have in the past. Like most consumers I am keenly aware of the game: the game that goes, "everything new is old again." Still I too am stuck in this rut just like all the other compulsive buyers and spenders. It has become a way of life that we somehow need a new car, a new fridge or a new pair of shoes. Occasionally, we convince ourselves that we must have a new love interest. But on this night I refrain from adding to the coffers of Macy's. I soothe my conscience with the unkind thought that they have probably made more money on this day than I've managed to earn in the last twenty years.

I know there is nothing old or wrong with the shirts I have in the drawer or stored away in a laundry bag crumpled and smelly. A little washing and cleaning would make them look just like the ones I am tempted to spend nearly a hundred bucks on just to eventually give them the same resting place as the old ones. Whatever!

It's a short distance to Broadway and as I get off the bus and go down the crumbling steps of the subway I remember briefly that when I first arrived in New York City at the age of eighteen years I did not know what the hell a subway was. But that was long ago and I was innocent back then, and maybe New York City seemed somehow more innocent. Maybe the U.S. and the world seemed innocent too. But before I get carried off on a tangent I return to my senses and get back to reality. I know that that this is only in my time. Perhaps there has never been any innocence here in this place with its sweat shops and its legend of slavery. Some accounts say that it was the last place in the north to officially declare slavery's end. No, this little piece is about me and this night in New York City in these times. I descend the stairs slowly. I am grateful that on this day at least the steps are not wet and icy and that there is no chance that a drunk will slip and fall again. The last time that happened was in January and his fall nearly broke my spine when both feet made contact with my unsuspecting rear end.

Now, some six months later in July, I swipe with my Metro card and enter the busy promenade to the sound of the rock band which has temporarily taken the makeshift stage. The singer is performing rather poorly a Bruce Springsteen song and I decline this continuous assault on my eardrums. Instead, I prefer to endure the cauldron commonly known as the downtown side of the subway. I know it's a poor choice for the ride but I have no other. The Number One train is a block away on 7th Avenue and it is just as hot there. I will take the "R" train and from this halfway house of purgatory I plan to ride it to my stop at the end of Manhattan. The station is insufferable and with temperatures that I am certain register 100 degrees F or higher, I cannot help but wonder how it is even allowed by the Health Department. I return to my senses when I recall that in winter the reverse is often true.

I continue a few steps to catch the front of train I pass the resident homeless man. He seems a kindly fellow and he always has a nod and a smile for me. I cannot help but notice that the legs of his pants are rolled halfway up and his calves and ankles are swollen beyond belief. I stop and speak with him, advising him to check into an emergency room if he has not already done so. He nods as usual and promises he will but I know he will not do so. As I leave him I thrust in his out-stretched fingers the usual three dollars. It breaks me up to see this and I can't help myself. He always seems so peaceful and grateful and it is a prize I have learned not to be ungrateful for in this town.

Continuing my trek to the front of the train, I am met by the sounds of a subway musician playing her guitar and singing. I've never seen her here before and I wonder why she has chosen what certainly must be one of the hottest nights of the week to demonstrate her musical talents. Knowing a little about the voice I am sure the heat is not favorable to her. I walk towards the bench where I plan to sit and rest my tired body before the train arrives.

But as I near the spot I come upon a scene I'd rather not be witness to. There is a man lying there and his bald pate is only rivaled by his bare behind which is planted in a position facing the pedestrian walkway. I turn my head so as not to seem disturbed and forgoing my original plans, I begin a hopeful prayer that the "R" or "W" train will soon arrive. Another five minutes and I am rewarded by my vigilance. The "R" train comes roaring into the station headed: destination Brooklyn, New York. In its progress there will be many stops and I will exit the train at the South Ferry/ Whitehall station.

I take a seat and prayerfully begin my short journey into abyss of one of the city's ancient tunnels. I have only to sit there for a minute before I hear the familiar sounds of the opera singer. He is accompanied by his boom-box blaring the classical violins, violas and French horn sounds atop which he adds his huge baritone voice. It is not an unpleasant voice. He is singing in Polish and I listen for a moment wishing I could understand it. He seems to have timed his performance and it is over soon enough. Before the train comes to a stop at the next station he stops singing. Placing his "orchestra" on the floor of the car he begins making rounds with his container cup. He is asking for donations for his performance and though tempted to oblige him, I think better of digging so soon again into my pockets. I ignore him. Instead I watch as he exits the car and heads for the one behind us.

As the singer exits and fresh passengers board, among them is a lean man of obvious Hispanic look. He doesn't sit. Although there are still several empty seats he remains standing. The newcomer is speaking on his cellphone and he is agitated. He is screaming into the phone as if his listener is stone deaf. I cannot help but wonder how he expects the conversation to continue much longer. After all it is practically impossible to get any telephone reception underground. But he screams into the thing telling whoever he is speaking with that he is on his way to work but he is delayed because the trains are late. It is probably a lie and I would come to wish he had not told it because two stops and ten minutes later we are indeed stalled at the Canal Street station.

We sit there as the lean man, whom I now notice is a user of some kind paces the floor of the car. He calls the job again and this time he asks if the boss has arrived there. He implores his listener to explain to the boss that he is now "stuck" between the station and the Canal Street exit. "These 'Bs' are not letting us off," he yells. His behavior is annoying to everyone on the car but although tempted I refrain from saying anything. Years ago I learned not to utter a word when witness to a scene where a man was exposing his private parts to a rider I was just seconds from interfering. Somehow, I refrained and when he exited the train at his stop I saw to my horror that he had in his back pocket a butcher's knife. So much for the city's slogan: "If you see something, say something! I remember that the saying, so popular only two or three years ago is no longer en vogue.

For the third time on this night the engineer announced that we were being delayed. Seconds later the engine shuts down. On the warmest night of the year, I am stuck on the train watching a mad addict pace the floor screaming, while above the din a couple are shouting at one another across the aisle about some mundane office experience. The engine has been shut off and along with it the air conditioning, and it is hot! We sit for another twenty minutes. I learn later that subway trains are started and stopped by a main control tower located somewhere in another Borough and that once turned off, the engineers are powerless to restart them. He has to wait for the tower to begin the connection. Well, at least now I know. Like I needed to know that!

At long last the train operator announces that we are again moving forward. The subway lurches into the Canal Street stop much the relief of most passengers and the opiate user. He de-boards the stuffy car but someone just as annoying gets on. She immediately announces her predicament. It seems she and her kids, wherever they are, have found themselves in a tight spot. Her husband has looked for work but has not been able to find anything at all. She feels the need to announce that only one of them can work because the other must babysit the kids. They'll do any kind of work to survive, she says: they have even tried McDonald's. They always use McDonalds as though handing drinks and burgers to patrons should be considered the ultimate comedown. I want to believe her but I find myself doubting her story. She appears to have rehearsed her little speech too well. I give her two dollars anyway, Just in case the part about the kids going to bed hungry is true,

By the time the train arrives at the Whitehall station and I walk up the short flight of cramped stairs I am exhausted and feeling like I have worked a second shift. But I follow the other lambs as we head up the escalators and the stairs to await the 8 o'clock ferry that will take us all across the salt water estuary to Staten Island. I've made it with about six minutes to spare before boarding time.

I am almost grateful that cell phone reception on the boats is poor. Most conversations will have to be shortened because about halfway across the waters the calls will drop. At least, I think to myself, I can close my eyes and drift off to the rolling of the waves as they splash noiselessly against the starboard sides of the "Samuel l. Newhouse" ferry boat. But I am wrong. It is announced that the next ferry to Staten Island will be loading from doors 1 and 2 and it will be the starboard sides of the ancient craft: The John F. Kennedy that the waves will be splashing against. I sigh and take my place in the line of late homebound travelers headed for the peace and tranquility of the last place in New York where hopefully at least for a few more months the rent will remain cheap enough to survive. And where it is not uncommon to begin one's day to the sound of crows and one's nights to the chirping of cicadas.

Heading for the corner seat that is almost secluded enough to hide one's presence and where through an open window I can almost reach out and touch the waters below, I am relieved to see that I've made it just in time. I throw my shoulder sack into the corner and half close my eyes. Suddenly, I am jolted by the sound of the hawkers. They are also on board and they begin their well-practiced spiel in unison: "Is there anyone on board who would like something to eat or drink. We feed the homeless and the hungry on a daily basis.

You don't have to be homeless to want something to eat," they chorus. They will take even a penny as a donation and to leave no possibility of a donation unexplored, they announce that they even accept kind words and prayers." Even though in the past I have witnessed the lead player in the group as he stopped at the Lottery counter and searched for coins from his "donations" to play his numbers, I decide to give a single dollar bill. I'm thinking that I might do better to keep the kind words and prayers for other more needy occasions. On this night I too could use the prayer part. A prayer to be left alone for just 25 minutes or until the J.F.K. safely reached the other side of these waters that boasts a depth of 200 plus feet.

For a brief moment I am lost in thought and I wonder what it must be like at the bottom. I wonder if we are really only riding the waters atop a huge mountain or a gigantic plain. It's a scary thought and I return to musings of a more tame nature. I try to ignore the incessant chatter and din coming from the throats of a few of the other passengers. There is a woman singing a song that sounds like a child's nursery rhyme. She is unrelenting and she sings it over and over nearly the entire trip. Of course there is security aboard; there is always a show of force on the boats but they seem unable to remind passengers to lower their voices or to respect the ear space of others. For the most part they behave as though they are really there for exercise as they stroll back and forth from one end of the vessel to the next and then back again. Their attitude seems to be that as long as there is no touching or violence involved they are content to just let things alone. It is rare that they are tested but tonight's ride will be a rare one.

It's getting late and I want to get home where I can stretch out on the bed and read or listen to the thumps of my upstairs neighbor who walks her floors as if she has ingots of lead attached to her bedroom slippers. And I almost make it. I say almost because with just a lap to go there is an argument between two male friends who can't make up their minds why they are mad at each other. It goes on and on until the ferry boat security patrol arrives on the scene and carts one of them away. It is revealed that the argument is about money and a "Doo-Rag". The more vociferous man screams that he has paid the other too much money for it: the price of forty dollars being too high for such a thin piece of a rag. He claims he has had better in the shops on Bay Street. Quite unwillingly he walks with the officers as he taunts the other man. "I'll be waiting for you on the other side," he shouts. "You forgot I know where you hang out," he screams. His voice can be heard shouting loudly even as the Captain of the boat announces that the ferry will be docking shortly and that all passengers must leave the boat. He then says that anyone wanting to return to Manhattan must enter the station and take the next boat. The JFK will not be returning.

This is not good news for those with no place to spend the night. I'd heard that it was once possible for the homeless to ride the ferries back and forth all night long. At least they wouldn't have to brave the elements. At least they could get some sleep in a relatively safe environment. But returning to Manhattan is a boon for the hoard of sightseers and tourists from abroad who run from window to open spaces searching for an advantageous position to take a great shot of the Statue of Liberty with their cell phone cameras. They'll push others out of the way and trample feet as they angle for an open space near a window. It's a free ride for them except for the subway fare and they are startled by that realization. Mostly, they talk loudly and fill the seats that might otherwise be occupied by homebound workers.

They chat in languages not understood or misunderstood by the locals and they point with admiration and pride to the marvel of the copper goddess. A symbol of beauty and grace, she is also a monument whose designers and sculptor borrowed from the obscure pages of Roman antiquity: the symbol of a harlot, a prostitute. She has been chiseled into a modern day symbol of freedom. Today, the statue, donated by the country of France, and upon which are written those immortal words penned by Emma Lazarus in 1875 almost seems a cruel joke. I wonder what thoughts the tourists and admirers would have if they knew the true story behind her beauty.

I think of the old song, "Will you still love me tomorrow?" Today, the year Eighteen Seventy-Five seems like a long time ago when she wrote: "Give me your tired, your poor, your huddled masses yearning to breathe free." Although both tired and poor and certainly living in Europe during those years, there is surely zero chance that any Black souls made the trips. For me, it is difficult to watch this without remembering that as arduous and uncertain as it must have been for those travelers, their journeys no doubt paled in comparison to those who'd made a similar journey under much different circumstances across Africa and the wide span of the Atlantic Ocean more than two centuries earlier.

I think again of the homeless and although the poem she wrote was not intended to be placed on this celebrated symbol of freedom, I wonder what dear Emma would feel if she knew that many European descendants of those huddled masses she wrote of are still tired and poor. They too have yet to benefit from the promise of breathing free, no matter how much they may yearn to do so. And that they are riding the trains and sleeping in cardboard boxes all over this city. They lie on sidewalks with swollen and dirt-encrusted feet and with infection- riddled legs; sometimes making a meal from the remains of food left in public trash cans? They too are still the "wretched refuse of your teeming shore." And I'll bet she'd be shocked to learn that some of the heirs of the very people for whom she wrote these noble words are now themselves standing tall: boots upon the necks of that "wretched refuse' and those un-freed souls.

I blink, realizing that this topic is also another story and I walk up the ramp and head toward the buses. That is, I begin walking until I hear the familiar voice of the gentlemen who cannot seem to refrain from asking for a hand-out each time we meet. He is polite and he calls me mister but I walk past him indicating that this is not the night. I vow that I will not dig for coins or bills into my pockets yet another time.

Mother Nature has prepared a great start to the night and looking east one can see the sky. It is a refreshing view that I did not have the luxury of seeing too often when I lived in the middle of Manhattan. I am grateful for it. But I am not grateful to witness the several bodies already stretched out on the hard benches preparing for their night of rest, I remind myself that providing the weather cooperates they won't need quilts and blankets for another four months. Here, the ferry platforms appear to be a favorite respite for those unfortunate enough to be homeless. It does not matter which of the four or five ramps one climbs to await the bus arrivals. There is always a homeless soul or more lying on the benches. Sometimes they've vomited their guts beneath them. The sight forces bus riders to turn their heads and bodies as we continue walking and standing until the buses pull into the slots.

Mine will be a brief ride and the bus will deposit me almost at my doorstep. I'm pleased digesting that little piece of comfort and while waiting, I take a seat on one of the stainless steel benches that have been put there almost as torture to tired travelers. These are one- inch wide steels slats on a backless frame. I am sure they only could have been intended as punishment to someone who has been very, very naughty.

The benches hurt and bring pain to the backside of anyone not born with a horse's behind. But I sit and I am rewarded for my stoicism by a homeless person who after begging for the small sum of five dollars paces the area in front of me. And then, while waiting for the bus drivers to pull into their places to open the doors, to our joint disbeliefs she pulls down her jeans, squats not six inches to my left and urinates! I was done and I get up quickly and hurry to the opened bus door, as the driver, still in shock, laughs and shakes his head.

Once on board I reach into my pocket to count. I am almost surprised to find that I've got twelve dollars and change remaining from my daily budget. I have given away about ten bucks and I feel almost guilty that I didn't help the last guy. But there is always tomorrow and I am sure he will be there waiting. Looking up I see the smiling face of the white woman. We ride the same bus most times and I nod. I have often helped her with the shopping cart she carries. She works somewhere around Wall Street and she is going home. Her composure is reminiscent of my former neighbor in Manhattan.

Also mature and Caucasian she worked on Wall Street and when she passed she remembered me in her will. This lady seems a cut from the same cloth. She is friendly and talkative and after complimenting me for yet another time on my attire, she asks if I too have worked late. I answer her but tonight I don't feel up to talking and I take out my cell phone, pretending to check for missed calls. She takes the hint and continues her knitting. She is always knitting.

It takes only three minutes before the bus begins to slow for the quick turn west on Bay Street and the stop across from the park. I know without thinking that among those waiting for the bus will be an assortment of drinkers, smokers, beggars and whores. It is like that every day at this corner. Situated just across the street from the park, in this section everything seems to begin and end. Even the small restoration that went on in the park barely two months ago has not slowed the traffic or eliminated the attraction this small area of Staten Island seems to have for those seeking respite and their own special brand of pleasure. It is close to my place but I don't go there any longer because incredibly, all the fixing up of the park seems to have only made things worse. No doubt the removal of the old brick comfort station that had become a haven for rats is an improvement. But the rats are still present in more ways than one.

There is a Pizza shop across the street that seems to be very popular and around the corner there is a porno store. I've never been inside either but it's not hard to imagine what is sold in both places. It is not hard to imagine what's inside the porno establishment because the owners have not been shy about their advertisement. There is a huge poster of a female on the door. She is fully clothed but her posture speaks volumes about her intentions. She is pictured standing just above a few steps and the message is clear!

Quickly, I recall my last visit to the park. I was there at the entrance while waiting for a bus to take me the few short blocks to the ferry station. Previously, I'd never before noticed that there appears to be greater interaction and mixing of the races going on there. I was not surprised that blacks and whites mix. This has always been true. Black and white friends and couples are kind of an accepted normalcy here on the island. But this was different. What I was now witnessing was a sort of comradery between Mexican and Black males. Albeit, the discussion I overheard had to do with money or drugs it was obvious that the three Mexican men who were being accosted and threatened by the lone black figure did not meet him that day in the park. I stood watching for just a few minutes as he threatened and slapped the beer can from the hands of one of the men. Standing only inches away he shouted and pointed his finger into his face. He then turned to the other two and screamed obscenities at both.

One of the men was trying without success to apologize but the Black guy wasn't having it. Mercifully, the bus arrived and I left the scene with the uncomfortable feeling that the immigration everyone speaks of is very much here and alive and that it is being further punctuated by the other "I" word: integration. I doubt seriously that this integration is what Dr. King had in mind when he spoke those words from his "Dream" speech some fifty years ago. Whew!

It had been a very long day. Unfortunately, it had not been an unusual day for me here in this place called Staten Island, New York. As I stick my key in the door and head for the relative safety and sanctity of my small abode I cannot help thinking that mine is a story not any different from those being played out in hundreds of places around the Boroughs of New York. Maybe it's always been this way. Maybe the homelessness and the open usage of drugs and alcohol are but symbols of the larger issues and not in and of themselves the problem. Maybe there has always been a blatant disregard for human sanity in this place that I have somehow managed to live in and to fall in love with all these years.

In my view what is sad about this story is that it seems to have no end. Of course, I know that there is a beginning which is symbolized by the border crossings of the "soi-disant" immigrants. I also know that those immigrants were all European. We've been reminded of that fact many times over in books and lately by a President. Nonetheless, it is a fine monument, this spectacular sight of the Statue of Liberty as she holds her torch high on Ellis Island. But it is not the entire story. That tidbit is glaringly interrupted by the black and brown faces one passes in the streets of the boroughs.

It is underscored and re-enforced by the chatter of the multi-colored languages that swirl around us like falling leaves on a breezy day in autumn. For myself, if for no one else I have come to grips with one poignant fact and I don't really give a damn if no one else agrees. There are not eight million stories in this, the Naked City. The old television show had it all wrong. There is but one story in this place called New York, New York and it all boils down to the story of the "haves and the have-nots." There is almost nothing in between.

Certainly, there are those like myself who may sometimes disagree and adamantly assert that being "different" and gainfully employed and useful to society we lie somewhere in between. We can pay the rent, the car-note, and the mortgage. With a few dollars in the bank and credit cards we can take an occasional vacation twice a year. We can even send the kids to school and put food on the table each day. But being one or two pay checks away from bankruptcy does not make us a "Have."

Alas, I resign myself to the realization that for the time being I will continue to pretend that I've "got it like that." I will continue to give, give and give. The choice is not mine to make and even when I suspect that I am being lied to or misled I give just in case. Like a friend once said, once you've decided to give it matters not what happens to the money: it's not your any longer.

So I must walk the concrete blocks and pass the faces of those looking for help. I know that theirs is not a contrived need of the moment. I get it that the issue lies much deeper than the desire for a drink, a cigarette or even drugs. It is one that will continue to rub shoulders with me and I am powerless to really make a difference. A few cents or a couple of dollars do not a millionaire make! Most of all I cannot ignore the faces or the voices I hear that pound upon my brain and my consciousness like the steady beat of the bass player sixty-five feet from me in the church I call "eglise de la porte panchee."

And I seriously doubt that when her friends championed for her words to be immortalized at the Statue of Liberty, it was never imagined that there would be peoples of other colors at the windows and standing in boat lines to catch a glimpse of the mighty monument. I doubt that anyone back then believed that one day her sight would somehow cause tingling to the spines of anyone who was not European. That they understood what those words could someday invite to future arrivals is unimaginable. Even though those future peoples might, through no fault of their own, take the words literally: "Send these, the homeless tempest- tossed to me."

Had they grasped the concept they might have insisted upon adding the caveat: "but not any non-Europeans and certainly not in such great numbers!"

And as for the lamp that is lifted beside the "golden door," well, that lamp is only lighting the way for very, very few souls.

For the rest of us, we must make do with a wooden door, a small candle and a leaning gate. Even then, a slight change in the wind and we might one day lament: "All Came Tumbling!"

Maurice P. Fortune

September, 2019

& ALL THRU THE HOUSE

IT WAS CHRISTMAS Eve at County General. With no one waiting at home and an almost hairless head bursting with a lifetime of memories, there was little point in hurrying. Walking the corridor on the way to the office he couldn't help the awareness that few people had bothered to come to work.

He might have guessed from those absent in his own office that the rest of the hospital would follow suit. A quick check of the clock on his desktop computer showed it was 11:45.

All the news that was fit to watch had been seen. He'd played the word quiz vocabulary, and would probably play again before the end of the day. Actually, it was fun. There were so many words to learn and it was always a challenge scanning through the synonyms and sometimes the antonyms of newly acquired words. He loved using the words as weapons. He'd trot one out in the middle of conversations with his peers or with a doctor or nurse, knowing full well that they hadn't a clue of its meaning. Then he would stand back and watch them squirm, pretending they understood or just gloss over it while not having the courage to admit they were at a loss.

But it always worked. Lately, he'd remarked how much respect and leverage this kind of knowledge provided him. Sure it helped that he was wearing a name tag, indicating he spoke French. Everyone it seemed wanted to speak French. Even those who spoke Spanish, the hospital's primary foreign language were somehow in awe of anyone who could boast of speaking French. Haitian Creole didn't count for very much. But if one spoke French then the usual questions followed. "You speak French," they'd ask? "Where did you learn it? Did you study French? Are your parents from France? Does anyone else in your family speak French?" He had grown weary of the questions and wished he could turn his badge around so that this information was not visible but this was not possible to do. It could land him in a heap of trouble because all employees had to wear their identification tags with their photos and their departments clearly readable.

Sitting in front of the computer for a few minutes longer he got up and headed toward the door. He stopped just inside the archway to speak with the young receptionist. She was Chinese. "Where you goin', Markis", she asked. He didn't bother to answer. She seemed to be a nice girl but in a way she was also kind of irritating with her mindless questions. She behaved as if she used others to continue bettering her command of English. A Temp, as her yellow name tag proclaimed, she claimed she'd arrived in the U.S. a year ago but her knowledge of English belied this. She even knew a bunch of slang words and there was no way she could have learned them and possess the ability to do so without an accent in just one year. Markis was no fool.

Learning English in China was one thing, but at that level. She was full of it. Also, she was no girl. She was, admittedly so, a married woman. In speaking with her privately she had on at least two occasions intimated that she now believed herself to have married too soon. She wanted to continue her schooling at a nearby University and work. There were contrary arguments with her husband. He wanted her to perform her duties like a good Chinese wife was supposed to do. She objected to this kind of "old" way of thinking. There had been vicious discussions.

There just happened to be another Chinese worker in the office. A few years older than the first girl, Markis had worked with her for four years, and he had had come to know a great deal about Chinese culture. She'd recently returned from a trip there. Although this time it had not been a pleasant one. Her father, sick from his travails with cancer, had finally passed away. She told friends that she had suspected as much. After all, how could she not have known working in a hospital and seeing day to day so many people in similar condition? She'd known that once doctors here refused to continue the rigors of chemotherapy, the trip to China to find someone who could help defy the odds was futile. She had, only gone along with the idea for the sake of her mother. But she knew. Alas, she knew in her heart it was over. This trip, she had come back with her usual trinkets and amusing stories if not her normal vigor. She had related how, in China the houses were extremely uncomfortable and cold. It was necessary she said, to wear coats inside the houses because of the temperature. It was something she was quite unused to doing. And the food was a bit tasteless.

Of course she was accustomed to the unhealthy fast foods of New York City but the change in diet produced minor health problems. Everyone laughed when she mentioned that at least her family was from the south of China: the north being famous for its menus featuring delicacies of dog meat. Everyone was surprised to hear that dogs are grown to maturity in pens. Sort of like chickens are raised in this country.

Markis thought no more on the subject as he continued down the corridor. He retraced the steps he had taken a little more than four years earlier. So much had happened in such a short time. So many lives ended here between these walls. So many newbies born. It felt like only yesterday that he had walked through the revolving doors and down the many steps into the vast space commonly known as the Atrium. Now, like then the entire area was decorated for Christmas festivities. People came from miles to take photos of the giant Christmas tree and the simulated snow that topped the roof gables of the old part of the façade.

The architecture was compelling and eye-catching. It had been designed and created with a stroke of genius and vision. Even now, some thirty odd years later one would be hard pressed to find its duplication anywhere in the city. He pondered this for a few seconds more reflecting on those times four years ago. Sometimes in life things happen that are meant to be. He had known the moment he walked through the doors that he would work there. No, he didn't know at that time it would take just a little over six weeks to go from volunteer to temp and then another two months to be hired permanently but he'd known he would somehow be hired. The coup de grace occurred when he showed up in the middle of an 18 inch snow storm.

No one else except the boss bothered to come in that day and that was the clincher. He had a job. And not a minute too soon because although he wasn't destitute, he needed to earn a living.

Markis suddenly became aware of an approaching figure. There was no doubting to whom belonged the bent frame and wearer of blue slippers. He'd seen her many times. It was Ms. K. She was often in and out of the hospital seeking assistance of one kind or another. Although she never took the advice of doctors, time and time again she returned.

Her feet were actually rotting beneath her and everywhere

she walked the stench was unbearable. This was not something of which she was unaware, and she apologized profusely. "I know they smell," she'd say "but I wash them and use the cream I was prescribed it just doesn't seem to help much. They wouldn't let me stay in the Shelter if I didn't," she'd repeat in all sincerity. He didn't doubt her. Once when Markis passed through the Port of Authority Bus Terminal he had come upon her sifting through garbage cans. It wasn't any wonder she was slowly rotting away.

There was no one in the hospital gift shop and few people walking the long corridor save the resident homeless guy. Seventy-one years old, he had a bed at Ward's Island but he caught the bus on time and returned before the curfew hour. He didn't like it but the place he lived in was much better than most, he said. And it was miles ahead of the shelter not far away. Theirs was the leader in filthiness, robbery, stabbings, assaults and occasional rapes. He no longer sold his wares across the street as he had in the past because the local police department had forbidden him to do so. After a night or two in the downtown jail he took them at their word. He normally liked to stop and talk a few minutes but on this afternoon, the eve before Christmas he seemed preoccupied. He could only manage a slight smile and a brief nod before he continued on his way.

For an instant Markis stood looking up at the tiers. He could see the clinics were practically devoid of souls on this day and he reflected on another time when he had seen it this way. It had been that way in the aftermath of Hurricane Sandy, when most of the clinics were closed for a brief period. It was cold then as it was now but somehow it seemed much more so. The absence of heat in the building and the darkness that prevailed, not to mention the fact that the hospital emergency rooms were shuttered and there were no in-patients added to the feeling of gloom. But the silence that prevailed throughout the building was bone chilling. It penetrated the walls and the ceiling. It echoed with footsteps on the stairs and in the emptiness of the corridors. No people, no lights, no heat, it was almost unbearable.

Those had been difficult times and when it was over there were those who actually shed tears. Well, he couldn't blame anyone for feeling that way. Standing there now his mind leaned back to the young Oriental girl who, finding herself with child and not wanting to bring shame upon her family, jumped over the balcony in an unsuccessful attempt to commit suicide. She had failed and the result was months and months of therapy to heal a body broken in pieces.

He wondered what had become of her. He noted that on this day all the emergency waiting rooms were completely empty. And normally, just walking these halls he was bombarded with greetings from staff and visitors. Some he knew, others he did not but it was always a feel good moment to realize that after only four years in this massive institution so many knew of him.

He returned to his office but at one in the afternoon he realized the moment had come. The time that no matter how much he wanted to he could no longer delay. It was time to take clipboard in hand, straighten his tie and head upstairs. All the way upstairs to the 8th floor and to probably the most difficult part of his job. It was time to see the prisoners. The island prisoners with their myriad issues and their problems that almost no one could fix. It wasn't that no one tried and certainly he did everything he could. It was the seeming futility of it all. He could not do anything about their legal situations.

It was an almost impossible situation to be in because when it came to the law many of the inmates were astoundingly astute. Then too, he was forbidden to make calls for them and any interpersonal contact was frowned upon. They were contraband. He had been told by his superior that detainees were hospitalized for medical or psychiatric reasons and sometimes both. And that was that!

But it was next to impossible for him to respect these rules and inevitably he would become involved in some small part of their lives. He had to admit that maybe sometimes the involvement was a little too much. But he was only human. Just interacting with them had forced him to learn as much about the law as he could. There were a number of codes governing criminal and mental health law and looking at an inmate's chart could tell you just about everything he needed to know before meeting them. There were 9.39, 9.37, 9.27 and 7.30 and then a list of sub-circumstances. All could get confusing but no knowledge of this could put one in a difficult situation because depending upon the staff in the forensics units to inform him that a prisoner was dangerous was something Markis could never be sure would happen.

More than once staff had let him enter an interview room with a dangerous person with only one exit possible. And to be in this predicament was unnerving. He'd had to think fast and maneuver quickly several times. But on this day, Markis would throw caution to the wind and he got a little too close to someone, well he had certainly done so before. And many others he got close to had never been to a prison. Besides, the guys on the forensic units seemed to like and respond to him. This was certainly the case with the first person he was going to visit on this Christmas Eve.

DELIBERATE INDIFFERENCE

Getting off the elevator he remarked how quiet it seemed. The usual hustle and bustle of guards changing shifts was absent. In fact, when he turned the corner he saw that there was only one armed person at her station. "Good afternoon," she greeted him. Smiling, he returned the salutation and placing his clipboard into the bin he walked through the metal detector. "You're good," she said, handing him his clipboard. "See, you later." "Merry Christmas," Markis answered softly. Walking to the gates in full view of the female guard seated behind the glass window he smiled again. She was a nice person. She always greeted him warmly wherever she saw him. In fact, all of the guards from the Department of Corrections were pleasant: at least with him. This was in sharp contrast with the hospital staff. Somehow they viewed his appearance as a threat.

But a threat to what? To their peace and calm and to their do-nothing attitudes? They eyed him suspiciously. Like they were expecting him at any moment to take out a pen and take notes. Or to record how disrespectful they were to the patients. How they positively ignored the approaches and questions of their charges. How time and time again prisoners reported they've been mistreated and then, fearing retaliation, begged for no action to be taken against the offender.

To some of the staff it was just a job. They come to work, nails freshly painted and wearing clothing designed to please the other sex, and sometimes the same sex. They'd already made up their minds what kind of people these prisoners were and nothing anyone could say or do would change their opinions. Few stopped to consider that in many cases the prisoners were their own worst enemies. Even fewer placed little belief in the prisoner's stories that they'd been assaulted by correction officers on the island.

Markis found their stories believable. How else could one explain several dozen prisoners all saying the same thing? All of them with the same fractured jaw injuries in exactly the same location and presenting with intense jaw pain to the Maxillofacial clinic. The injuries were not only similar but appeared as if someone caused them to happen in the exact spot over and over again with different prisoners. It was difficult to ignore that there was a method and a lesson in the madness.

There were also those who were there because they were victims themselves. Sometimes they inflicted harm upon their own bodies in any number of ways. There were those who had tried suicide in various forms. There were cutters, or self- mutilators which took the form of slicing the arms, legs and bodies with sharp objects. Not enough to kill but enough to cause scars and great pain.

There were genital mutilators, anal mutilators, bleach and caustic substance swallowers. There were those who'd swallowed sharp objects or pushed them into their rectums so that bleeding occurred. Then, of course there were those who harmed others. There were the reportedly unprovoked lashings out at strangers in bus terminals, train stations, on the street, at school, at church and in stores. But even these crimes, usually classified as a person who is a danger to himself and to others, rarely merited the disrespect and abuse they suffered at the hands of all who would later come in contact with them.

Occasionally, a provider was callous and showed these prisoners no regard as human beings. Markis had been told that this or that person was a drug-seeker or a malingerer: a trouble maker. And even if some of this were true one could hardly place blame on the person. A hospital bed was a great deal more comfortable than a three-inch mattress on a hard surface on an island. Who would not malinger?

The only interaction with the law Markis had ever had was the time, many years ago, when he had been briefly arrested and charged with the Misdemeanor. The arresting officers, both wearing plain clothes, had handcuffed him with his hands in front. The suit jacket Markis was wearing was put over the cuffed hands. Once inside the Precinct he had been placed in a 6 X 9 holding cell and given a chair to sit. All of this was the doing of his rather tough and experienced attorney who, after taking one look at the bullpen with 20 to 25- odd faces hopefully and expectantly peering from behind the steel bars, announced to the female guard that his client was "not going in there." "Why not," she had asked rather belligerently? Mercifully, the Captain intervened before there was serious confrontation between the two and nothing further was said. Markis went to the holding cell amid the cries of protestation from the bullpen occupants. In the end he had been released in his own recognizance.

Signed in 1791 Amendment 8, to paraphrase, has three principle features. It deals with the rights of all prisoners in the United States to receive free health care, being unable to pay themselves for these services. The second and third parts treat excessive fines and excessive bail. The intent of this Amendment of the Constitution, like the Constitution itself, was undoubtedly meant to serve a different population.

But over the years, mostly due to the growth of populations in the cities, fueled by events like wars and the end of slavery, things changed to suit the burgeoning United States of America. Now, well over 200 years later, most of the prison population in the U.S. are non-white and poor. WE'VE COME A LONG WAY BABY. The overwhelming majority of today's prisoners, as every schoolchild knows, are proportionately black. The crimes rarely fit the punishment. Nonetheless, unless we are going to scrap the Constitution, States and Federal Governments are bound to uphold the law. And the number one issue Markis was concerned with on this day as he prepared to enter the jails or what he'd come to refer to as the 'forbidden zone' was the first part of Amendment 8.

Markis waited patiently at the 2nd check point. He was always aware of the cameras, even though he couldn't see himself, he knew they were following him. Finally, the guard opened the gates to allow him entrance, Markis walked quickly, expecting to wait again at the next gate. He passed a small corridor of of holding cells. Each was about the same size as the one Markis had briefly occupied those many years ago. There were always flashbacks at this stage of his visits to the jails but despite the flashbacks he walked on rather cheerfully. After all it was Christmas Eve.

He hadn't expected anyone to be in these cells but in passing he heard someone call his name. He stopped, as if riveted to the floor.

The voice called again. "How are you doing?" Markis had seen some strange things in passing through this area. There was once someone who decided to void his intestines on the floor of one of the cells. He said he kept calling the guard to take him to the toilet. After calling out for an hour and being ignored, he had taken matters into his own hands. Then there was the fellow who had undressed himself and stood at the bars making obscene and inviting gestures to all who passed. Markis had heard he'd been redressed and beaten by the guards for his lack of control. Markis had never mentioned to anyone the time he passed by one of the cells and had witnessed someone masturbating. What would have been the point in reporting such a mundane occurrence?

As he turned toward the voice Markis recognized the caller. The voice belonged to someone who had hoped to be at home with his son and his wife.

The wife he now suspected of cheating on him. But alas, he would be spending a few more Christmas' behind bars. He was to have gone to court three weeks earlier. In fact, he had gone to court and lost. Putting on a cheerful face, Markis approached the bars. "Hi!" He couldn't say Merry Christmas. That would hardly have been appropriate. "Why are you here? Are you alright?" Markis asked these questions almost in one breath. "I'm okay, I had a clinic visit," the prisoner replied. Markis could see by the exposed wrist and forearm that the wound was healing well. The tell-tale scar would remain forever, unless Plastics would agree to hide it.

Markis knew that this was considered elective surgery and he knew it would never be done at this place. Even at the age of 41 the man was an exceptionally good looking person.

He must have been a lady-killer, Markis surmised. During an earlier visit he'd told Markis, of a wife and son. The son was older than 18, Markis was certain of this because he could not otherwise be considered as a proxy. He had been reluctant to name the wife. Was she actually his married wife? Now, surrounded by two other detainees in the cell, with each hanging on to every word passed between them, with questioning glances the conversation between Markis and the man was brief. He knew that the cellmates were trying to find out what they could discover. Anything incriminating to be used against their "homie" at a later time. The two were careful not to divulge anything. "I have the copy of your health care proxy which was returned by the post office," Markis ventured. "Oh," he replied. "Let me give you a new address.

I wanted to ask if you could do a new proxy just for him. I don't want to use my wife anymore." The prisoner's statement dripped of bitterness. "Sure, Markis said. "I have a form right here, all you have to do is sign it. I'll make copies and mail one to him. I probably won't be able to get back here before you leave today but if you send me your address I will mail you the original." "No problem with that. I still have your card in my Bible. I always keep it with me." He said smiling. Markis completed the formalities, asked for permission from the security guard who had come closer to hear everything that was being said and then handed the form to the prisoner. He was careful to maintain eye contact even though he knew this might be taken to mean intimacy by his cellmates.

With the formalities completed Markis quickly said goodbye and walked away. What a rotten way to spend Christmas, he thought. The man had told him why he was in prison but all Markis could remember about the conversation was that it had something to do with marijuana selling. They were small amounts. Amounts of an illegal substance that just a year later would not have sent him to jail at all. And what about the enormous amount of money he'd claimed had been advanced to the attorney by his wife? Somehow the figure of twenty-five grand stuck in his head. Did the woman ever really pay this money to anyone? The amount seemed exorbitant.

It was possible to stand at the final checkpoint gate and still look into the faces of prisoners in the holding cells. Markis was tempted to turn and wave a last goodbye to but he thought better of it and waited until the guard with a bunch of keys tethered to his belt finally came to unlock it. He was the same guard who always looked at Markis as if he was seeing him for the first time. He gave the impression that he had as much interest in the job as he might have in throwing himself off Niagara Falls. Markis repeated the usual greetings and this time he added Merry Christmas, as the guard mumbled something back to him.

On this unit one might find anything and everything. There were those who were here for medical reasons and those who were psyche patients who needed medical attention. He shivered when he recalled some of the horror stories he'd heard. One man had hardly a space on his body upon which he had not taken out his frustrations and vengeance. He proudly showed the scars to everyone, claiming he could not help himself. He was always afraid the next cut might be a deeper wound to the neck and his last, but what could he do? He believed himself powerless to stop cutting.

Markis had once seen a man, also an ex-con and a paraplegic in the Emergency Room. He had been refused admittance to the hospital where he could lay up for a few days. He had cut himself in front of police at the Port of Authority Bus station. Returned to the hospital by ambulance he had been treated and discharged. When he called the office for help Markis had responded to the call. There was little he could do for the man and becoming angry the man took a sharp object from his pocket and in front of Markis and other witnesses he slashed his arms with it. And if that were not enough, hospital police, nurses and doctors were unable to stop him. When it was over he was treated for his new wounds and once again discharged.

Yes, this was County General's Forensics Units with its plethora of patients who would do anything to escape their imprisonment. This was mostly at the island facilities notorious for its stabbings and "lock in sock" fights. Its vulgarity and sometimes its rapes. Markis had seen prisoners brought to the units who had ingested sharp things: nuts and bolts, shards of plastic, bleach and other caustic substances. They would put things in their ears and their rectums too. Anything to get off the island for a few hours or days. But there was also another sinister side to their desire to come to the hospital and with no proof Markis had kept very quiet about it. He had been told more than once by a prisoner that he wanted to be discharged from the hospital because his mission was done. He had come to pick up a package of drugs and now that he had it he would return to the island to make money, lots of money. Markis could only guess where the package was being stored until the discharge took place and there was only one guess necessary. More often than not these were only runners. The middle man with the intended owner of the package safely awaiting the 'goods' on the island. On this island with its illustrious history of being one of the training site for Black American Civil War Soldiers of the Northern States. How shameful!

Once inside the gate the first stop here on was always at the Nurse's station. He didn't go there to check in or to receive orders. He already had a census sheet that he'd printed out from downstairs and there were rarely bed changes. Some of the prisoners, those seriously ill, are kept here seemingly forever. Occasionally, they remain here until the take the last breaths and just for a moment Markis thought of his first introduction to this place. At the time, Forensics was not a part of his patient schedule. But if someone happened to come into the office needing assistance or guidance the department was always available and on a day, less than twelve months ago such an occasion arose. A man walked into the office while Markis was seated at the reception desk answering the phone. The man, an ex-con himself Markis would learn, had a brother in County General. The brother was ill and he was serving a life sentence in a prison.

The patient was having difficulty and could no longer ambulate to the Day Room to watch television. His brother, who had not seen him since coming home from prison wanted to do everything possible to make life easier for him. It was clear that life had been hard and now that the final act was being played out in a hospital bed; he was dying of an illness for which there was no cure. He had months, maybe minutes to live. Markis had done everything possible to assist the man and a slew of arriving relatives. The brother was now spearheading the drive for better care. Markis had called and spoken with the Deputy Warden, the Director of Medicine, the people in Risk Management but the answer was always the same: No television service for prisoners, dying or dead it made no difference. Nothing seemed to go right for the man in his last days, even his petition to be released from jail on humanitarian grounds was, at the last minute denied.

Time passed and Markis had not seen the brother for a couple of weeks. Unexpectedly one day he appeared in the office again. This time it was to thank Markis for all he had done to help and for a second there seemed to be a glimmer of hope that the story would have a happy ending. But the man stated rather in a- matter-of-fact way that the brother had passed on. It was a very awkward moment before Markis was finally able to say I am sorry. The brother continued, asking for a sense of direction to find some group, anyone who could help prevent his brother from going to Potters Field. Markis obliged, giving as much help as was possible and the man left the office without a goodbye. He said he'd return one day but he never did so.

He walked quickly to the nursing station. Not because he was in any hurry to see the two or three people whose names he'd set aside but because he wanted to avoid meeting his nemesis: the Director of the unit. He was the main reason Markis had come to the jails at this late hour of the day. He had promised one prisoner, a paraplegic young man that he would stop in just to hear his story. It seems he had been taunted and threatened by the Director who had told him if he continued complaining he would be shipped back to the Island. This was the usual practice employed by the person Markis was rapidly losing respect for as a professional. In this case it was downright harassment because he knew well that his target, suffering decubitus ulcers on his bottom and needing at least another week to successfully heal was totally at the mercy of the institution.

But the unit needed the bed. It was a special bed fought for and won by the patient after a series of telephone calls and numerous letters written to government support agencies. The patient, in this case was a smart guy. He was well-spoken, well-written and read but surprisingly not a university graduate. It was like that with some of the prisoners. They could absolutely stun you with their knowledge on many subjects, the least being law. But in addition to being well versed this prisoner was a charmer and possessed great charisma. He had worked hard to overcome his handicaps. He knew he'd never again use his legs. It was sad that he was only 35 years of age and a former dancer. Markis was in admiration of the guy who might in the end lose the other leg as well. Still he persisted in building his upper body strength.

Working alone, he had achieved great things and for someone his size and in a wheel chair he would put many body builders to shame. He knew it and flaunted it, refusing to wear even an undershirt to hide his prized chest, flat stomach and well-built arms. Markis secretly believed he was envied by the infamous director: hence his antagonistic attitude.

No matter the crime they had committed, or the seemingly senseless situations they found themselves embroiled in it was almost impossible not to like some of the prisoners. They were often personable, intelligent and kind. He walked to number forty-six and stood in the doorway for a moment observing the scene and waiting until he was seen. Markis was stunned by what he was witnessing. There was a tray of food thrown in the middle of the floor and bed A was in total disarray. The person who occupied this space was sitting on the exposed toilet. His flesh was wrapped around the tiny toilet seat like an oversized hamburger on an undersized bun. Looking as if he was in another world, he too was well known to Markis.

This was a young man, rather large and extremely volatile when he was upset. And he seemed to become upset with the slightest provocation. Markis immediately understood the conversation he'd heard between the female Captain of the guard and two inferior officers. "We can find other ways of dealing with these people besides what you are doing, "she had said. Her tone implied that she had just witnessed a struggle and the placing of hands on someone. She continued, "I am not putting up with that shit, not on my watch, and I'm not tolerating anymore of his fucking tantrums either." Both of the male officers remained silent as all three turned to look at Markis when he excused himself and pushed pass them. They all looked down at the ID. badge Markis wore hanging from his neck. They said nothing. The badge gave Markis the right to be there in any situation.

"Mr. Markis," the prisoner greeted him. "My man, thanks for coming I knew you would be here," he said again. At first Markis though he was referring to the fact that it was Christmas Eve but he soon realized that the man had called the Office while Markis was on his way to visit the unit. He had called to report that the young man in bed A was being beaten by the officers. As they talked the young man stood up from the stool. Without shame or reservation he wiped himself in full view of both on-lookers. Then, he pulled up his pants and charged out into the corridor yelling and screaming as he went. Pretending not to notice what was going on, Markis listened as the prisoner continued the conversation.

"I told you," he said. I try to help these young guys but they don't listen. They calm down for a few minutes and then they break again." Markis didn't respond. He was thinking of another roommate he had seen the last time the man was in the hospital. It had been just a few weeks earlier. The roommate at that time had not been young. In fact, he was an older Spanish speaking man who only knew a few words of English. He had tried to advocate for him as well because of the lack of care the man was receiving.

The man, practically comatose and lying in a fetal position, had also had his rights championed more than a few times by this same prisoner. Markis smiled at the comparison of the two roommates. He knew the man had a heart as big as the room and it didn't matter at all what or who was receiving the injustice.

He did not like it and was bothered by it. "I love that suit," he remarked. "I can't wait until I come home. I am going to take you shopping with me so you can pick out my clothes. How many suits, do you have? I bet you don't even know!" Markis made no effort to respond. He knew that although the man was hopeful that a video of the crime scene would help clear him it was the only thing he could hang his hat on. The awful truth was that from the story the man had told there was no certainty that this evidence would even be admissible in a court of law. There were so many variables and the attorney had not been bothering to return the numerous calls placed to him by his client. They chatted for a few more minutes before he knew he had to press on to other patient. When he said goodbye in a moment of softness and said, "Yeah, I got my day dreams." There was no need to say more. Markis understood and turned and headed for the door.

There was a momentary commotion at the other end of the corridor but obeying the number one rule of his department he did not investigate. He was in Department of Correction territory and he had no purview here outside of violations by hospital staff. Whatever was going on at the other end of the corridor he did not need to know to do his job. He did note that he didn't see or hear the voice of the roomie.

Nearly through the check point gate he realized he had forgotten to visit an inmate. He was also a paraplegic with extremely thing legs showing beneath light blue pajamas. He had a sad face and eyes brimming with expectancy. This guy was eager to talk and at the last visit Markis had almost had to pry himself loose from the incessant chatter. He was waiting for the second of his planned operations. The first operation had removed two very large kidney stones and several small ones. This was worrisome to the man as he had been in pain for more than two weeks but the pain seemed to be worsening. Especially when he lay down at night. Sometimes, he confessed, he cried himself to sleep. Markis suspected he cried for other reasons too but he did not respond.

Making a mental note to try to get back to the unit to say hello he walked through the second check point. Hurrying to the nursing station he noticed that the guard with the keys, a rather short Black American woman with short natural hair, looked at him in an odd way. She looked like she'd wanted to say something but having changed her mind she'd decided to hold her tongue. He thought he knew why. He believed at the time she might be trying to make a pass at him. He was used to it, it happened all the time.

Wherever he went in the hospital he got compliments on his clothes, on his respectful way of approaching others, on his youthful demeanor. And it wasn't always just the women. More than a few men seemed for whatever reasons to believe him hot. He had been called a "catch" by more than a few but on this occasion he could not have been more wrong about the intentions of the guard.

"Hi, I'd like to speak with Mr. E. H." He announced this to the head nurse. "Is he available?" It was one in the afternoon and at that time of the day some of the inmates were being medicated. Celexa, Depakote, Ritalin, Lithium, Ativan, Klonopi, Risperdal, Prozac, Adderall, Zolox, Zyprexa. These were the weapons used here to fight mental illness and aggression, irritability and substance abuses. Most of the prisoners were awaiting trial or had been tried and not sentenced. All had varying degrees of mental illnesses or substances abuses: cannabis, heroin, cocaine, K-2 addiction, alcohol. At least that was what their charts read.

He knew their diagnoses by heart. There was schizophrenia, paranoia, depression, altered mental state, unable to care for self, a danger to self and others, cluster B personality traits, bi-polar, suicidal ideation etc. etc. Some were extremely dangerous and could explode at the drop of a hat. Or, sit in quiet- smoldering self-destruction. Others were zombies who walked around talking to themselves, their code was named preoccupation.

They were sexually preoccupied, religiously preoccupied and so on. At times these preoccupations led them to do odd things. They attacked strangers on street corners for no apparent reason. They lashed out at friends and relatives, teachers and cops, mothers and significant others. To the untrained like Markis, they sometimes made perfect sense while at other times they ranted on and on with ideas of grandiosity or reverse feelings of worthlessness.

Markis knew a little about these things because a beloved sister had undergone years of these sufferings. She succumbed to her illness. She had been beautiful and seemingly lived with the world on a string. At least until it all collapsed. It had taken years for the end to come and not all of these were bad years. But the result had been the same. She had been one of the patients who had been given the now rare electric shock treatments.

On this unit these inmates sat talking together in small groups. Sometimes they paced alone in the corridor. Sometimes they menaced others when they didn't get their way or just because someone got in their 'way.' It was almost a veritable zoo and the only thing that distinguished these patients from their peers on the other psychiatric unit floors below was the ever present fact that they were considered criminally insane. And the staff was themselves an odd bunch. Save keeping watch over their charges there seemed not a lot to do. Employees sat in the corridor on chairs waiting for something to happen. Waiting for a prisoner to 'go off" so they could intervene. Ostensibly, to protect the patient until the crisis management teams were called arrived to administer the required intra –muscular injection. This was the medicine over objection shot that all patients hated but immediately tranquilized and put one into a state of peaceful oblivion. At least until the next outbreak.

The bare truth was that some of the staff appeared to actually enjoy administering their own brand of pain medicine in the form of physical abuse.

As much as they disliked the nurses and the guards the prisoners hated the injections even more. Some felt that acting out gave the sitters an opportunity to act out their own aggressive behaviors. They punched, kicked and twisted limbs all under the legal guise of getting the situation under control. At first Markis didn't want to believe what the inmates were saying. But the several times he had seen these staff in action had convinced that all of the prisoners who reported having undergone this torturous treatment could not be wrong. There had even been deaths on the unit.

These were mysterious death for which no one was ever held accountable. There were inquiries and meetings of the heads and important people. But in the end all was neatly smoothed over, covered up and written off as necessary action taken to protect the lives of the others. The deceased was no longer a danger to himself and others. It would no longer be necessary to place him in the "quiet" room. He would now be forever quiet.

"You might not get very much from him today," the nurse said. She was almost smiling. "It doesn't matter," Markis rang back at him. "I just need to know for the record that he is safe." "Well, good luck with that," the nurse replied. He was unable to hide his joy at the thought that he could make someone uncomfortable. Turning, he called for an escort to accompany Markis to the patient's room.

Markis walked with the escort not knowing what to expect but was pleasantly surprised to see the man sitting up in bed with a sheet over his head. He didn't want to talk and Markis knew better than to insist. He'd learned from experience that it was always best to leave the person alone and to try another day.

Usually after a few days they would come around and have something to say to him.

As Markis turned to leave the room a voice said to him, "what about me, don't you wanna talk to me?" "Of course, I want to talk with you," Markis instinctively said. He turned to look at the speaker and came face to face with a very young face. He was shocked by the young man's youthful appearance. A fair guess would have put him at 15 or 16 years old though Markis knew he had to be at least 18 to be there. Later, Markis would learn the man was 20 years old. "And what do you want to talk about," he asked.

The young man indicated he did not want to speak in front

of the escort but when the escort would not move. He blurted, "I DON'T WANT TO LIVE ANY MORE!" The absolute finality of the statement stunned Markis and for a moment he was unable to respond. In all the trips to these forensic units Markis had never encountered this. He could see quite clearly that the young man was not joking and he hesitantly asked him if he would like to talk about it. "No," the young man said. "I am doing everything I can to die. I don't take my diabetic medications, I don't eat and if they give me pills I try to hide them so I can use them to overdose. I really want to die," he repeated. "Well, you might want to die, but I want you to live," Markis told him. "And I will be doing everything I can to make sure you live." With this the man turned his back and returned to his bed leaving Markis no choice except to walk away. "I'll be back," Markis promised. He didn't realize how soon he'd return. Markis would learn later that the young man was in prison because he'd gone to see his mother. She had refused to see him or even talk with him amd he became abusive. She called 911 and the result was that he'd been arrested for abuse and disorderly contact. His mother already had a restraining order against him, which his presence violated and that was that. He wanted, so desperately just to speak with his mother and be forgiven and given another chance: just one more chance. But she refused him saying that he'd had many such chances and now it was up to him to finish school, get a meaningful job and contribute to the family. "How can I do any of this?"

His eyes brimmed with tears. "I don't have a place to stay. I can't live in these dirty shelter places where I get in trouble all the time. People are always trying to game on me and I don't like it. I like it better when I'm by myself," he said. The last comment was an afterthought.

Walking back to the gates Markis could hardly contain himself. He stopped briefly considering placing a call to the man's psychiatrist or at least alerting the head nurse on the unit but he knew from past experience that nothing would get accomplished this way. For one thing, the head nurse seemed preoccupied and probably couldn't care less what happened to the young man. And he had been trying to reach doctors all day long. But what was to be done to help this person? What could Markis do? As he waited at the gate he pondered this question.

He hadn't noticed until then the small six-foot Christmas tree. It appeared haphazardly set up in the corner for the staff. It only could have been for staff because it was completely beyond the view of the prisoners. Although they might catch a glimpse of it as they entered or left the units.

The short Black American guard walked over to let him out of the Unit. As he thanked her she seemed to gain impetus from his words of holiday cheer. "Can I ask you a question," she asked. "You don't have to answer if you don't want to but"…she hesitated as Markis assured her that it was fine to ask. "Why do you come here?" Markis had not expected this question. "I come here because this is part of my tour and I have been assigned to these units by my supervisor." "Oh, I know that," she replied with words dripping of disdain. "But, these people are murderers and thieve. They hurt other people and then they come to prison where they are treated better than the victims. Where are those who are helping the victims?" Her statement reeked of sarcasm!

Markis tried hard to be nice. He explained that prisoners have the same rights as everyone else and generally gave her the humanitarian spiel but the woman was insistent. Markis even assured her that there were victims service offices right there in the building just a few floors beneath her. This stopped her briefly and she pretended to be interested in their telephone number. She feigned writing it down and told him that when she retired she would start a victim service of her own. Markis told her that it was good idea. He knew she was full of it. He imagined that she or someone she knew had once been a crime victim. She seemed so bitter.

As Markis walked away he added the guard to the list of those who believe prisoners are sent to prison to be punished rather than as punishment. He silently wondered why anyone with such bigoted ideas would choose to work in a setting where daily they must come face to face with prisoners. As he walked away he thought, people will do anything as long as they get paid!

There was a lone woman in the tiny waiting room and she was crying. Some prisoner's loved one who had been denied a visit. Hadn't she known that visits are only permitted on certain days? She probably thought the authorities would make an exception on today, Christmas Eve. She might have guessed that they never make exceptions. Never, ever!

Not visiting a unit was something he rarely did but it was sometimes unavoidable. On occasion he didn't have time but in some cases it was simply the wrong time to visit. These were during medicine times and staff meetings, recreation times and group therapy times. Or, like today when an inmate became too much for the staff to handle alone. It was not a pleasant thing to watch as the offender fought against the injection until he was pinned to the floor or bed. It took a few minutes for the sedative to kick in and one could stand outside the frosted window and watch the 'downed' individual slowly slip into "la-la land."

They used the same method elsewhere in the hospital or whenever anyone was out of control. It was legal to do this and sometimes necessary. But people had been known to become very ill following such injections. Markis had once attended a meeting where someone bravely discussed using a mattress or other padded protection to corner an inmate and pin the offender to the bed. He had wanted to ask, "For the safety of whom?" The poor prisoner could have been smothered to death. But, to save his hob he had wisely kept his mouth shut. He had heard that one could be barred from attending such meetings for insolence. Or, blackballed if doctors didn't like one's comments, or clothing or for almost any reason at all. It was a privilege to be invited into the in- circle.

Just as he had made up his mind to forgo the third unit, he noticed that the gate was actually opening almost inviting him to enter. It seemed the guard had been watching his progress and anticipated his visit. He waited until the guard finished reading his ID. As the gate opened to the fourth and last checkpoint Markis walked to the nursing station. He did not particularly like the staff on the unit. They all seemed to come to work just to sit on their behinds. They showed nothing but a cutting dislike for the patients. They justified their feelings and comforted themselves by judging everyone there: painting them with the same broad brush. Staff believed all were criminals and incorrigibles.

The doctors, particularly the chief had an attitude that dripped with disdain. She was tall and thin, with a face set with eyes of steel. Any hint of prettiness was forever marred by a thin and grim mouth set in the angular face. To add to her cold image she possessed a voice that was borderline shrill and very much nasal. She was cold. The staff knew it as well as the inmates and they all hated her. In fact, everyone believed The Sphinx of Egypt to be far warmer.

But today, as luck would have it she was there, in the nursing station and much to Markis' chagrin she wanted a word with him. Graciously, she invited him to sit but he remained standing while she gave him the heads up about an inmate who had asked to see him. Markis remembered the last time she had given him the heads up about an inmate she deemed harmless. He had spoken with the inmate in a private interview room and had almost to flee for his life when the man, a six foot three or four, two hundred eighty pound giant stood over him and began seeing Markis as the enemy. Even though there were 3 or 4 guards just outside the door Markis had had been quickly forced to invent the excuse of needing to get a pen to write the man's complaint.

He'd left the unit shaken that day and did not return the next. "I just wanted you to be aware that this person wishes to be addressed as Ms.", the stone-faced woman said. She seemed to delight in saying it. "And she has a card you gave her when she was last here two or three months ago." Even though the unpleasant voice kept speaking he did not hear her. His heart sank and his mind raced. Of all the people he had hoped not to see again, this was the person. Not because of her sexual identity. It had nothing to do with the fact that he now chosen to be identified as she. No, it was because of who she had been rather than who she had now become. How could he have not known? He did not remember seeing her name on this morning's census. Maybe it was there and he'd overlooked it. He managed to ask Ms. Steely voice for an escort. He thanked her and left the station to visit the patient's room. But as soon as he stepped into the corridor he came face to face with the patient he had hoped to avoid.

She didn't give him time to ask any questions. She behaved as though she had been anticipating his arrival. Like she'd rehearsed what she had to say. "I need a sports bra because my boobs are hanging and I am getting too much attention on this unit. I don't belong here and I don't know why they keep doing this to me." This was a stretch. The last time he had seen her she had asked him for a pair of sweats. At that time he had patiently explained that items of clothing are the purview of the Department of Corrections. He had been able to get her double portions of food but not much else could be done for her. Now, two months later she had returned and was asking for the same thing. He could not help seeing that her boobs were hanging.

It wasn't any wonder that she was getting attention from the other inmates who were all males. There were about forty of them from all nationalities and all walks of life.

And she was being housed on the unit because regardless of what she called herself she still had male genitalia. Markis wondered if she knew. Did she know that Markis knew her identity? Markis bet she did. Although several years had passed since he had seen her. The last time had been when he and her father were shopping. That had been about 10 years earlier and it had been at least 10 years before that when they had first met. Markis understood that there was another family. There were brothers and maybe a sister or so on the mother's side. And then there was the father's side.

He took another long look at the now fully grown person in front of him, the eldest son of his friend and Markis was perplexed. He wondered why she didn't just come out and tell her father the truth. Without bothering to check the records he thought he knew why she was there. She had again taken scissors or knife in hand and tried to eliminate once and for all her remaining genitalia. She was one of those who self-mutilated. Markis had heard through the grapevine that she was also a prostitute. At six feet tall and at least 220 pounds she was a handful to say the least. Except for the effects of the hormone shots that had obviously softened her body and the large imprints of boobs at her chest she certainly wasn't very feminine looking.

She tried to raise her voice a tone or two but there was no mistaking the masculinity.

He had been tempted to speak with her father and let him know the truth bur he knew that this could never be seen as correct. It would be a violation of the HIPAA Law and one would be fired on the spot for that. He could never morally approve of telling this person's secrets. Her father would have to find out on his own or remain forever in the dark. He knew full well that given her reasons for being there, prison officials would never entertain the idea of a razor, even a safety razor, but he would do everything he could do to secure the double portions of meals. She seemed otherwise content but Markis wished there was something that could be done to help her accomplish her dream of becoming a full-fledged female. He'd wanted to tell her, cutting off one's private parts was not the answer.

He stood in the corridor listening patiently to her pleas for double portions of food, and a razor to shave the growth of hair that was accumulating on her face and probably her chest Markis realized there was precious little he could do to help. He decided to end the conversation and play it safe. Pick another hill to die on a friend had once told him. He promised to address each request and then saying Merry Christmas to everyone he passed Markis headed toward the steel gates.

Sometimes, just coming to the forensic units was pleasant. The inmates overwhelmingly approved of his presence and would line up expectantly. They'd ask, "You here to see me?" Even when he was not there for them he'd tell them yes and then take time to carefully check their names off his bed list. He would listen to their complaints and wishes. For the most part they wanted to know their discharge dates. It was difficult to say he couldn't possibly divulge that kind of information. But to their credit even when they didn't understand, they would remain respectful of his presence. Today had been an exception and he almost regretted coming.

As he waited for the elevator to take him back to the office he lost himself in thoughts of the first day he'd walked through the revolving doors. His thoughts went back to that first experiences and he realized that he had never really learned to separate his professional personality from the private one. The advice he'd received during that first month echoed in his brain: "Never let them change you!"

Markis still considered those words and replayed them occasionally in his head. The advice had come from an unlikely source. A patient he had met on another floor. Markis never really understood why the man was there. He was also too naïve to look at the patient's chart and now, he would never know. The man had been young, from the streets and obviously a hustler. He had begun by asking Markis to bring him small snacks to his room and Markis obliged.

Even when he escalated to newspapers and magazines or a few dollars Markis continued to indulge him. Then, one day he realized the patient was calling him two or three times each day. In fact, so much that the other employees in the office had noticed the calls and had become suspicious of the man's true intentions. Markis decided he had to end the relationship and he pondered it for a few more days. But he continued to provide the snacks and to cater to the whims of the requester. An unpaid volunteer worker at the time, he received only a small unemployment check, the relationship was hurting Markis' pockets more than he was willing to admit.

But something kept him going. Something he didn't understand. Then, after three weeks of this the patient announced to Markis that he was being discharged in a few days. Markis was of course happy for the man as well as for his own pockets. He didn't really care what the other workers were saying. In fact Markis knew they were probably right. On the last day of his hospitalization the patient called Markis to his room. He invited him to sit beside him on the bed but Markis declined saying protocol would not allow that kind of familiarity with a patient. As Markis stood the patient poured out his heart. He spoke of an aunt who lived uptown. Only a few blocks from where Markis was living with a brother and his wife. The patient requested a health care proxy be filled out for his aunt and Markis assisted him. When he returned the man thanked him. He looked Markis in the eye and in what was probably a rare display of genuine feelings he surprised him by saying with candor and honesty: "never let them change you!" The next day the man was discharged. When Markis went to the unit on his regular rounds he discovered the room empty. It was a Friday and the rest of the day seemed long.

As Markis sat at his computer on the following Monday a middle-aged black woman walked through the door. Markis had a sinking feeling in his gut and he listened as the woman requested property information from the director of the department. He heard her say to the woman, "Mr. Markis was working with him, maybe he can shed some light on what happened to your nephew." The woman turned to Markis and spoke of her nephew's sudden appearance at her home. She had given him ten dollars. He told her he was staying in a shelter and had come to visit her because he had no money. Leaving her home he had returned to the shelter. On the following day she received a call from County General hospital. Her number had been listed by Markis as the proxy and next of kin. He had been brought back to the hospital unconscious. He had expired!!

For a long minute Markis sat there staring into space. He hadn't heard much after that revelation. The woman said goodbye and Markis sat there for what seemed like an eternity. He finally excused himself from the office to take a walk. Like now, it had been late in December. As Markis walked many thoughts came to him. Of course he had been devastated by the news of the man's death even though he did not know him personally. But he'd been happy that he had not given up on him. That he had not denied him a few small comforts. But most of all he was still haunted by the depth of the man's advice: "Never let them change you!" Even now, four years later as he walked the long corridor back to his office he thought of the words and they echoed with each footstep. Footsteps seemed to speak to what he now planned to do.

The office was bustling. Several people stood crowded around the reception desk seeking answers while others sat at the two or three student desks. Desks provided for the writing grievances against various services in the hospital or an occasionally rude employee. Markis almost didn't notice the two women sitting closest to the conference room. Employees of interpreter and information services, he was glad to see them. It was part of his plan to get many signatures on one of the Christmas cards he had bought at the gift shop and these two would certainly help. This one would be given to the young man whose mother wanted him to complete school so badly she'd decided upon tough love: in the middle of a cold winter she kicked him out in the street. His colleagues were good about writing short messages. They used his first name and wished him well. Markis alone signed the other cards but he felt he the youngest needed a special boost: a little hope, a hug, a reason to want to live.

As the clock ticked fast toward the end of the day he began the walk back to the main hospital building. Somehow, the building seemed almost empty. He saluted the few well- wishers he passed but the throngs of pedestrian traffic normally crowding the corridors were noticeably missing. Hurrying past security he took the elevator. It was then that he remembered he needed to make one last stop and he got off on the 16th floor. A nurse, one of his favorites, had called him about a new admission on the unit who was giving everyone hell. Walking fast he stopped at the nursing station and asked for the heads up. When Markis heard the room assignment his heart fell. This was the 4-bedded space where it seemed all the troubled souls ended up. It was where the homeless Eastern European guy had arrived with an army of suitcases and bags. So many bags that Markis had been compelled to get other staff in removing the eyesore. It had become a health hazard. This was a patient who had very serious medical physical and psychological problems. He was obstinate and disrespectful to everyone but Markis had not allowed this kind of behavior from him and it turned out it was exactly what he respected. Even so Markis wondered what he was facing.

This patient was the most vulgar and paranoid Markis had ever encountered. He trusted no one and depended upon everyone. A man in his late 30's who had been shot by cops on two different occasions, he was paralyzed from the waist down. He'd been in and out of various prisons from New York City to the west and he admitted to Markis that there was not much he had not seen. "I can do nothing to defend myself." And he might as well have been quadriplegic for all the good his hands were. He could not grip even a cup or a glass of water, brush his teeth, scratch himself or lift his arms to accomplish even the simplest task. He told Markis that when nurses were upset with him they would scream at him and return his obscenities word for word. "You can't even wipe your own ass," they would say! Of all the things anyone could say to him this was probably the worse and the words would set him off like a match to gasoline. He would carry on in such a way that he could only be quieted by calling the crisis squad.

This was a patient who believed that everyone was secretly wishing for him to die and he feared death more than anything. He believed nurses were secretly plotting to poison him or give an overdose of medication. In the weeks ahead the crisis team would be called dozens of times. On this day, his first or second in the hospital, he claimed that after an ugly exchange with the patient in the bed next to him, also a paraplegic had asked a nurse to heat for him a cup of coffee and when it was given to him he threw the hot scalding coffee into his face.

This was the story he related to Markis who agreed to call the hospital police and to file an assault grievance. But the story was unbelievable. It was a stretch to understand how a paraplegic who could not move could throw coffee but to prove his case the patient had refused to have his bed linen changed until Markis arrived to witness the evidence. And there were indeed wet stains of coffee on the pillows and on the bed sheets. Disbelieving as he was it was his job to take the complaint as the patient related. Silently, Markis thought that as the patient slept one of the nurses had thrown the coffee.

Markis listened, recording everything but occasionally putting in a comment. As he listened he understood that the patient was born in Africa. He had arrived in the States as a young person and after a tough street life here he had turned to a life of crime. Bud even this hardened soul had an Achilles heel and his story was hard to ignore. It was a heartbreaking story of being chased and nearly fatally shot by gang members. He was offered placement in a witness protection program but in turn for his testimony against drug dealers but he had not felt it safe enough. Someone had discovered his whereabouts and he'd had to flee the city. He tried to begin a new life in Ohio but even here he was not content to live quietly. He'd gotten involved with drugs and was shot a second time. Although he hadn't had to flee for his life, his mother old, ill and tired asked him to leave. He boarded a bus back to New York City and kept clear of Brooklyn and the Bronx.

Hearing this Markis realized that despite his troubles and the turmoil of his past the man was full of life. He was still hopeful of starting afresh for the third or maybe the fourth time.

He asked Markis to hand him his cell phone. Painstakingly he dialed a number and after speaking briefly he handed the telephone to Markis, announcing in a quiet voice, "it's my mom, please say hello to her." The patient had a new champion for his rights and a new friend and ver the next two months the new friend's patience would be tested again and again as the patient, possessing no other weapon besides his mouth exploited the friendship. And he spared no one. Doctors, nurses, social workers, cleaners and his peers were all subjected to his vitriolic outbursts.

He would promise Markis that he would behave and then break is word again and again. He cursed and belittled everyone. He spared only his new found friend. But with all this in the future, Markis was able to soothe the patient's fears,. Markis said goodbye as he left the man and then Merry Christmas to all the staff he met as he hurried to the elevators to take him upstairs to the Forensics units.

The elevator was empty except and stepping off at his floor he walked quickly to be screened for entry. The pleasant woman with the nice smile was working and Markis was grateful for this stroke of good luck. She never asked him to go through the detector or be scanned with the hand scanner unless she was being watched. He thanked her, smiling when she commented on how conscientious he was to come to the prison on this day.

He had brought along an extra card and he was pleasantly surprised when to discover that the one he had helped complete a health care proxy was still there awaiting the van to take him back to the big island. He was a clinic patient and he'd said earlier that he was eager to return where he had a few friends. Markis had also brought along a copy of the health care proxy and he asked the guard if he might hand it to him along with the opened envelope containing the Christmas card. To his astonishment, the guard, not bothering to examine the contents allowed it.

Markis handed him both and said Merry Christmas to the two other occupants in the cell. He could see the happiness in their eyes. But both men were aware that they being carefully watched by the two cell mates. It was understandable. They were more than a little surprised by Markis' gesture of support and they searched the eyes of both men for anything they could read into it. Some sign of a past relationship, platonic or otherwise. Some indication that the two men might be somehow emotionally involved but they were mistaken. Anything, they could store away use later against would serve them. They continued to watch closely as Markis said goodbye and headed for the third checkpoint. Ten minutes later they would still be watching when he left the unit.

Seeing him standing there brought the usual broad grin to his face. "I was just sitting here thinking about you," he said. "I guess I must have been wishing on your presence pretty hard," he added laughing! "I guess so. I guess I heard you," Markis answered, giving him a fist-bump. "I'm not going to stay, I just wanted to say Merry Christmas again and give you this." He gave him the card. There was silence. The two men stood there as the last remaining sunlight cast shadows across the room between Markis and the bed where the prisoner sat propped up by two pillows. It's funny, Markis thought, how the most beautiful and peaceful moments find themselves cast in a glimmer of sunlight. He gave him the card. The patient's face had undergone a change. The smile was gone and there was a sob in his voice as he spoke. "You're gonna make me cry." He read aloud the card and then the few words Markis had added in his own handwriting. The two men remained silent as the last sunlight cast a final shadow across the floor. Markis stood at the window guards for a few moments more before leaving. He'd written on the card, THE BEST IS YET TO COME! There was nothing more to say. Wanting to show his gratitude he noted that the other occupant in the room had turned the opposite way in his bed. Markis gave another fist-bump and walked away. He was a fighter. Markis knew this just from the little victories and concessions he had managed to gain in just a few months. He'd insisted on a special bed and got it. He was adamant about a special cushion for his wheelchair to help prevent the recurrence of decubitus wounds and he had written to almost everyone in the government: City and State. He was tough and smart but Markis worried that he was too trusting. People could be deceptive, pretending to help even while plotting to destroy you. He'd wanted to say this to the patient but he was afraid to dampen the man's spirits. After all, it was Christmas Eve in the world. It is a tough job, he thought to himself.

Managing to keep his composure he walked past the holding cells where the first prisoner sat awaiting his exit from the unit. "I'll call you," he said. "I always keep your card next to me." He said this loudly and it appeared he had abandoned all pretentions and care for the thoughts of his two cellmate listeners. "Markis returned the smile, "I'll be listening out." It seemed odd coming from him, saying it this way, but he knew he had to at least try to sound street- smart. It was an old trick he had learned from being around the few souls from the street that he'd known before taking this job. He'd learned their lifestyle from talking with them and from being around them.

Of all the units in the hospital the next stop was the one he most hated. And this was not because of the patients. It was well understood that they needed help. And unlike the others these patients didn't necessarily pose a threat to anyone. Not that they couldn't explode and cause harm. Just reading their records confirmed that they all had that potential. But so have hundreds of others Markis saw riding the subways and buses or walking the streets of New York. Just that morning on his daily subway ride to work he had witnessed two women going at one another for no other reason than leg room. "It's not all about you," one had said to the other. "Get over yourself," she added. For a moment it looked as if there would be a brawl right there on the "D" train between 125th and 116th Streets. But all was settled and the two glared at one another until one disembarked at the 59th Street and Columbus Circle station.

What made this unit different was the fact that the hospital employees were almost all uncooperative. They seemed to truly believe they were doing these prisoners a favor by showing up each day. And there was one who seemed to take exception to Markis' presence. "These folks sure know how to call their boy!" Markis had heard him say this on more than one occasion. Well, their "boy" was there again and nothing could be done to prevent him from doing his job. Markis waited for the guard to unlock the last barrier.

Inside, the corridor was alive with patients. There were those who liked to put on a show. Whenever he came they would suddenly appear in front of the glass partition of the nursing station. Others paced the corridor. They would walk in and out of their rooms or into the day room. Sometimes they'd use the opportunity to start an argument or a brawl. But this time he had no trouble finding the reason for his visit so late in the afternoon. His reason had seen Markis as soon as he walked through the gate. He approached him asking "you here to see me?" When Markis answered that he was indeed there for that purpose the young man walked toward the end of the corridor where 3 or 4 officers from the Department of Corrections sat observing them. Markis had not intended to sit and talk but he felt he had no choice. Maybe, he could convince him to take his diabetic medication.

Seeing him coming one of the officers got up from his front row seat and opened the interview room. He sat the inmate on one side and Markis on the other. There was a table between them. Markis turned on the light in the room. He let the officer know that he felt safe enough to close the door. He also knew that the young man would never open up as long as he thought someone might overhear their conversation. "I just came to check on you and to give you this," he said as he handed the young man a red envelope. "What is this," the young man asked? He was apprehensive? "Oh, it's just something I want you to have. A kind of present." Markis answered.

He opened the envelope. Taking the card out he began to read. His lips moved slowly. "Who are these people," he asked as he looked at the signatures on the Christmas card and read the well wishes? "They're people in my office downstairs," Markis replied. "They spelled my name wrong," he said in a quiet voice.

He said nothing more. Markis eyed him steadily, not knowing what to expect. He wondered if he had made a mistake in bringing a Christmas card.

Finally, the youngster spoke. This time it was in an almost childlike voice. "Thank them for me," he said. "This is very kind of you, and I won't forget it." He got up from the table and left the room. He left the door half open behind him. By the time Markis left the room he had disappeared. Markis turned to face the officer outside the room but something stopped him short of asking questions. Instead, he bade him a Merry Christmas and walked toward the exit post. On his way out of the unit he passed the dayroom. He saw the young patient standing in the center of the room holding court. In his hand was the red Christmas card envelope. He seemed the perfect picture of happiness. They made eye contact but he didn't wave goodbye. He would learn later that the very next day the patient began taking his medications. He began eating once more.

The work day at an end Markis walked slowly back to his desk. Almost everyone in the office had gone home to begin their celebrations. Christmas parties had been celebrated earlier in the week and those who missed the parties at Christmas would try to catch those of the approaching New Year. When he looked at the mounting pile of documents on his desk he decided he couldn't walk out and leave them. He searched for any e-mail and voice mail messages he hadn't seen, heard or forgotten and spent a half hour or more closing out a few of them. Tiring of this he checked the upcoming weather report. He wondered how he'd spend his own Christmas Day. To be sure he didn't have any plans and with Christmas gifts bought for the god kids and his sister-in law depleting his extra cash he couldn't do much even if he'd wanted to.

But it didn't matter much. This year Christmas fell on a Thursday and he'd be back to work the day after. What was there to do? Markis put on his coat and headed for the door. He was alone in the office. This is how it'll probably end for me. Maybe it would be just as a song writer had written: Alone again, naturally. Smiling he left the office through the back door.

There were more people in the lobby than Markis had imagined there would be on this night. Most were visitors taking camera shots of the large Christmas tree. It was well decorated. Especially with no electric lights to brighten it. Whoever had done the job had done so masterfully. They'd succeeded brilliantly in bringing the Christmas spirit to this sometimes sad place. He'd heard that the tree and the backdrop were famous. They had appeared in magazines throughout the world. He paused for a moment to look back at the scenery. To look back and marvel once more on the brilliance of the architecture and the designers who had so successfully married the old façade with the new.

It was almost possible to imagine himself a few hundred years ago. To think of himself anywhere else except in a hospital. It was truly story- book and except for those souls still upstairs on the forensics units or, on their way back to an island. Except for those souls walking around the Port of Authority poking through garbage cans for treasure it might have been. Markis pushed through the revolving doors and walked out into the frost-bitten night air of the main boulevard.

Epilogue

As the days and weeks went by with new forensic patients arriving Markis found himself involved with new situations. They were new but they carried in so many sad ways the same old stories. Even with these new involvements he was constantly reminded of the one special Christmas Eve. And of those main players to whom he'd wanted so desperately to give some small measure of hope. One called on the phone requesting small favors. A message for his provider. A telephone call to his mother. He wrote to Markis. He used the name and address of one of his prison peers. One bitterly cold morning in late February Markis arrived at work, and in checking the census for the forensic units he was greeted with knowledge that he was once again admitted to the Medicine wing. After a busy day he finally got a few minutes to visit. He found him sitting up in bed as Markis remembered he liked to do.

But this time there was something missing. It was a more somber and pensive man in the bed this time and Markis could sense there had been a change. L.H. admitted that that he was tired of the letter writing and of pleading with his attorney.

He said he had dismissed the man because he had not done anything to help. L.H. said he could not understand why, with all of the technology available and the supposedly video camera shot of his absence at the crime scene, he was still in prison. He said all they had to do was check the camera tapes at County General Hospital. These he said would show clearly that he was there at the time the crime allegedly occurred blocks away.

Markis wanted to believe L.H. he hoped that he was telling the truth and that his imprisonment was all a terrible mistake. It was difficult to stand there listening and hear his lament of how much he missed his mother and his two children. He seemed so proud that his son now wanted to go on to college somewhere in the south. The two men talked for a long time with Markis standing at the foot of the bed and L.H. speaking in quiet and measured speech. It was almost a relief that his team of physicians arrived. Markis took his leave, promising to return the next day. It was sad to hear L.H. speak as if his conviction was now a forgone conclusion. He was already speaking of taking his case to the court of appeals. He was still speaking of his dreams.

The case of the handsome A.M. had not turned out much different. On a clinic visit he told Markis that in just a few days he would be facing a judge to determine if he would be receiving a penalty of 10 years imprisonment or less. It turned out that his court appointed lawyer had done nothing to help him. The bail was still $250,000, no small amount and there was not a soul he knew who could afford such a sum. There was also a surprising coincidence in the case. One day Markis received a call from a woman who identified herself as the fiancée.

Recognizing the woman's voice but unsure he listened as she told him that A.M. would arrive at the prison hospital on that day and was requesting to see him. At the end of the conversation the woman began laughing and the much to Markis' shock she said, "You don't remember me but I am the mother of G.G." Markis nearly dropped the telephone for G.G. was the young prisoner who for a brief time shared the room with L.H. At least until he'd erupted on that Christmas Eve and thrown his food tray on the floor, finally charging down the corridor to be handcuffed, screaming and kicking. His mother was the fiancée of A.M. Markis could scarcely believe it and when the woman finally hung up he looked up the health care proxy A.M. signed on that eve. Sure enough the woman was who she said she was, Markis noted in disbelief. What a tiny, tiny world, he thought to himself.

As for E.H. his story goes on. Markis learned that he had been discharged. But not to the streets or to his mother's home, as he had so desperately wished. E.H. would not be serving any prison time Markis found out. Instead he was sent to State. Being sent to State seemed cruel in the case of this young man but perhaps in time he would overcome his demons and be released to live a full and fruitful life. Markis certainly hoped for the best for E.H. At twenty he had so much potential and so much more living to do.

And for the paraplegic prisoner B.T. with the filthy mouth he so effectively and regularly used as his sole mechanism of defense. After the Social work department had worked tirelessly to find him placement in a number of nursing facilities he had been returned from each within a day. At last they were able to find him a bed in a home much further south. But to everyone's chagrin B.T. vetoed this place too, and then one day, quite on his own he wheeled himself out into the bright sunshine morning of approaching spring and disappeared into the city streets until the next visit to the hospital. They always come back to the County.

Finally, as if a cruel trick of fate played the final trump card, Markis would encounter one day the transgender son of his good friend. It was an unexpected meeting which took place in the corridor of the forensic west unit. Markis had gone there to deliver a copy of another prisoner's complaint. He became aware that he was being watched and he when he turned he looked into the face of the trans- person. After a brief exchange Markis was asked for the same help he had been requested of on the three previous meeting. He wanted double portions of food, a razor with which to shave the four-day growth of beard fast accumulating on his chin and a sports bra. As in the past Markis told him he could help with nothing except the request for extra food.

The rest was beyond his doing. As he took leave of her Markis could not help but sense that the entire conversation was a ruse. That he was being asked these requests not out of need but out of curiosity. This person wanted to know if Markis recognized her for who she truly was. Moreover, if in that recognition Markis had divulged the secret of her desperate and repeated desire to change gender without the knowledge of her family. In later checking admission records Markis discovered that she had tried once again to relieve herself of her private parts with a razor. Markis had already determined he could never betray that trust.

END

CUT THE RAP

ALMOST ON CUE it begins. Not softly, like someone is trying to adjust the volume. Not tenderly, as though an attempt is being made to 'spect the rights and ear space of anybody or anything living within a few hundred feet of the sound. That would be too humane, too respectful. It's always LOUD and it is always WRONG. Most of all it never fails in its 'tended purpose. And that purpose is to annoy the hell out of me. Me, Benjamin Polk Taylor the young septuagenarian who is try' to live out the rest of my days on this planet Earth in peace and quiet. Now don't get me wrong. I am not 'gainst peoples enjoying demselves.

And most of all I ain't against music. Any kind of music is alright with me. I enjoys it all. Even if I can't love it all or understands it when it's sung in another language. I have put up with classical music and pop music and Chinese music and Island music. It's all good to me. After all they say that music soothes the savage beast. "Ain't that right? Well, ain't it? Don't even try that s… with me. I know you got your own preference in music just like everybody else. I sure got mines. I tells everybody, don't y'all be a callin' and botherin' me no Sad'ys b'tween 10 A.M. and 2 P.M. 'cause I'm listenin' to 88.3 FM. That's that Rhythym Review Show that come on WGBO from Newark, New Jersey. Most of the week they plays them Jazz but on Saday mornings they plays them old songs from MY time and I just loves it. 'Course the Jazz is alright too. I'm glad somebody got sense enough to keep our black history 'live."

Listen! The ONLY reason I'm telling my story is because I don't want other folks to have to endure the pain and agony I've had to put up with during the last few months in this place. Now I been here for mor'n twenty years and I have NEVER had a problem like dis before. Nooo, not me! I seen 'em come and I seen 'em go. Some been put out, throwed out and carried out in body bags. I guess that's how I'll leave here one day; in a body bag but it's alright with me. When you gotta go you gotta go. Why I remember the time they found poor ol' Mr. Jamison in apartment 2- E. He was almost rotted away. And that damn Doberman pinscher that he kept to scare away the crack heads was so hungry it had started to tear away at his master's body. I'm telling' you the truth, it made my skin crawl. That's why I would never have a dog in the house. I wouldn't want to leave it to fend for itself and I sure as the devil wouldn't want it eatin' me up in my own house. That it is if I had my own apartment to myself.

But I'll get to that part in a minute or two. Then, there were the Taylor's. No kin of mine and that's for sure. They was always fightin and cussin' and carrying on. Why it got SO bad that the tenants committee had to go to Court to have a Judge kick 'em out of here. Not that I had anything to do with it. Oh, I was IN court every time dey called the committee. But I didn't have a damned thing to do with the decision to put them out. The only thing I ever did was sign the petition like everybody else. Well, almost everybody else. That f'ing woman Ms. Hudson wouldn't sign. She tol' the head of the committee that she was a Christian woman "God don't like ugly," she told him. "You'll get yours because you don't have the right to judge nobody, and that's written in the Bible." I think she was right on that score and anyway people who live in glass houses ain't got no right throwing stones. We ALL know that but I signed the paper anyhow. And I outlived mostly everybody else who did too. Even though I sure as hell can't stand to have no stones thrown my way? Yeah, I done out-lived them all. 'cept maybe those who moved back down south years ago. Like Peggy and her husband Don.

I heard they're still kickin' and doin' just fine. But I'll get to that in a minute, just hold on, I'm going to put down as much as I can because I'm not one of those people who just talk 'n talk. When I have a problem I think about it and I DO something about it and I'm sure as life planning to do something about that damn rap music, Excuse my French! I'm kind of taking my time here 'cause just in case 'dere's some sort of 'taliation I want to leave the police some good leads on just who might have been responsible for my early demise. If'n you get my drif'. To underline my position, I just want to mention that one crazy tenant who tried to hustle the landlord. He owed millions in back rent. That was doing those times when you could keep going back and forth to Housing Court with one excuse or 'nother. The plumbin', the 'lectricity, rats and roaches. You could use almost any excuse to keep from paying the rent and the Judge would give you a postponement. Why it could go on for years and meanwhile you could live rent free just promising to pay. Well, this guy, who like I said, owed a ton of money told the Judge that he was 'spectin' to get a huge settlement from a car accident he had three or four years back. He said then he would pay ALL the back rent. And the Judge believed him. Over and over the case was postponed 'til finally he was told that he had to come up with some of the money or bring a letter from his lawyer stating the reason for the delay.

When it come time to go back to court he showed up with a paper in his hand. It was s'pposed to be a letter from his attorney but it was all ripped and torn and the judge couldn't read it. His grandkids he said had stayed at his apartment over the weekend and they went into his papers while he was at the barber shop. The little one found this one letter and taken her crayons and was trying to draw pictures on it. There, he showed the Judge! Anyways, the other small one was jealous and wanted to draw too so they started fighting over who drawn the prettiest picture. Dey was pulling the paper back and fo'th 'til it was practically destroyed. That was why there were some sections missing. But you could see at the bottom that the letter was from an attorney's office. HIS attorney's office. He hadn't had time to pick up a copy but he would be sure to get one if the Judge would be so kind as to extend to him just one more month.

His Honor took the letter and looked at it carefully. Certainly, it was illegible. Nothing could be seen, well almost nothing. Casually, he asked the con man a simple question. What was his lawyer's name? I forgot what he said to the Judge but he couldn't come up with a name. He hadn't thought that he would ever be asked THAT question. Well, the Judge said his story was not credible because the signature at the bottom of the page bore the same last name as the landlord's representative. And when he showed it to the landlord's attorney he verified that the letter had come from his office. Nothing else was readable but the dumb ass had not thought to cross out the signature at the end of the letter. He used the letter because he knew he had to produce one from a lawyerses office and dat was the only one he had. Needless, to say he was issued an immediate eviction notice and he was out of the building in three days.

But getting back to my situation here. I just want to let the world know that I have tried everything I could to be a good neighbor to dese people. But dey just won't stop. They just won't Cut the Rap. It goes on and on and if it's not coming from one apartment it's comin' from another. And not just played. They sings to it too. I guess dey dancing too but a least I don't have to see that part. Why I guess they'd have to carry me out of here on a stretcher or in a straitjacket if I did. The boomin' starts early in the morning before the kids go to school. Course it's worse on then days when there ain't no school. Holidays and stuff like that. Oh, they sings too: the kids. Dey little voices, soundin' like Alvin and the Chipmunks. I can't understand how they manage to learn every word of these dumb songs but they can't learn dey lessons at school.

That is when they goes to school! An' if that ain't enough, they starts up again with that nonsense the minute they walk in the door every afternoon. It goes on non-stop all evenin' long. You know what really makes my blood boil? It's the fact that as bad as the kids are, the grown-ups are just as bad. If not worse. You'd think they'd know better.

But they don't. Or, maybe they don't care. Yeah, that's what it is. They don't give a sh... Why am I saying that? Why? Well, I'll tell you why. As soon as the kids are out the door in the mornin' and I'm tryin' to catch up on a little of the sleep I done missed the damned thing starts again. Oh, it's a different kind of music to be sure but it's just as LOUD. Now, I love Lionel Richie's music. He done written some good stuff and his voice ain't that bad either. I could listen to Toni Braxton all day long. Toni, now man that's a piece of meat and then some. I ain't gonna lie. But why can't they play the sh... for themselves? I mean, turn down the volume. I still can't see what they get from ALL them bass and drums. I think they use some kind of system call woofers or something. I got their damn woofers alright and it's hanging right here. Oh, I don't mean to be nasty about this but that sh... gets on my nerves and that ain't no easy thing to do. I'm pissed off about this whole business because it don't make no damn sense.

It don't take much to give a little space to one another. But you got to GIVE respect 'norder to get it back. At least that's what I was always told when I was growin' up. Anyway, music going day and night. Night and day. How's a man supposed to get any rest? I told you I think dey doing this just to get under MY skin. Just because one time I called dem cops. You gotta understand that I done tried everything else I could try. Just to give you a 'xample: some used to call out the window. Just like the girl did that time when they was havin' that birthday party upstairs. It was about 2 in the morning and the music was blastin'. It look like the party was just getting' started. But it weren't 'cause I know for a fact that I'd been listening since 'bout 9 o'clock myself. Anyways, she yelled out the window "cut it down or cut it off!" "Nothin'! Nothin' at all happened!" They just kept up with that crap. 'Bout ten minutes later she yells out again. "Cut it down or cut it off!" And this time they actually turned it down. I mean they turned it Waaay down! It set me to thinking', well, if that's all I have to do then the next time I'll do the calling out the window myself." But just as I was fixin' to relax and rest my eardrums it started up again. And the first song they played was MURDER SHE WROTE!

Well, when I picked myself off the floor from laughing I decided that maybe I was going 'bout it the right way after all. I sure as hell don't need nobody takin' out no contract on my behind, old as I am! Well, I'm not like those people who call and don't give their names. And I sure as heck don't call that other number they calls the quality of life number or something like that. When you do that they figure you not really upset about the noise. You just want to make waves. Well, I don't just wanna make no waves. I want the s… to STOP. Cease and desist as they used to say when I was in the war.

Yes, I called dem cops. And I give them my apartment number and my FULL name. I told them I was Benjamin Polk Taylor. T-A-Y-L-O-R. I told them that I live in apartment 21-B on the second floor of this place and I'm fed up with the disrespect. Sure, did. That's what I told 'em. I was so mad I'd have called Mayor Bloomton or da President if I'da had their numbers. And I said I didn't care if it was a holiday weekend or somebody's bar mitzvah. If they didn't come soon I'd take matters in my own hands. And I wasn't bull crapping. I think that's more the reason they came so fast. They thought I was some kind of nut or something.

I told the Sergeant that I didn't mean no harm to no one on the face of this Earth. I wouldn't hurt a fly but he acted like I, me Benjamin Taylor had committed some kind of crime. Like I was the perpetrator. They put a stop to the noise though. They went into the perpetratorses 'partment and told them they had to tone it down. Then, they showed them just how high they could turn the volume up. The cops have a measurement for that sort of stuff I know. You see I used to be 'round law enforcement officerses myself. Well, not me directly but my best friend Sammie did and that was just as good. You know Sammie who fell dead on the subway tracks a few years ago. Rest his soul. Not talkin' 'bout the dead. Well, brother was an auxiliary cop or something and he told me some good stuff about New York's finest, which I won't indulge. Or, divulge excuse me. Like I said, they interrogated me to no end and dat's da reason I never called again. And I STILL ain't to this day. I swear. Even though they 'cuse me of it sometimes. No, if Ben Taylor ever calls they gonna know it, 'cause I'm leaving my name, address and social security number too! I might even leave my hat size if they'll take it.

It didn't matter though. It was just a couple of days befo' dey started up ag'in. I 'member the time 'cause it was right about then me and that chick Shirley had a fallin' out. Everybody know who Shirley is. Well, everybody who's swinging if you know what I mean. She the one who's always hanging around 'bout the first of the month when the rest of us ole cats get paid. Not that I see nothing' wrong with that. It beats goin' down town on the train looking an' lookin'. After all, I still 'member what happened to Sammie. But on this day, I was determined I wasn't gonna let no broad take all my money.

I don't care HOW GOOD she looked. And she looked pretty good to me that day. And she know how to get to me too. With those big- ass chest and that camel butt. Man, man, man, oowee ! Well Shirley, she come up to me standing in the lobby. I had just got back from the store where I bought a little taste for Shanequa Pullman up on the 4th floor. It's one of her kids who keeps smoking that stuff in the hallway and leavin' all that cigarette tobacco on the floor for the handyman to clean up. I done heered him complain about it plenty times.

Shirley come up to me with an' starts her cooing and oowing like a cat in heat and I'm already ready an' jumpin' if I can USE that term, but you know what I mean Anyways I told her. "Girl you got a lot of sh… to you." And she lick her tongue out at me, then she put her finger in her mouth and asked me what I was sceered of. Now Shirley, she know what to say to you.

I was getting weak too. I ain't gonna lie! But I knew that I had already promised to spend the afternoon with Shanequa and I couldn't 'xactly break my word. Could I? 'sides, I was getting a free meal, a free movie AND some sex all for the price of one pint of Absolute! If that ain't a sweet deal I don't know what is. Maybe she ain't got the body parts built up like Shirley and her sex ain't nothing' to write home about but she can sho work dem lips of hersn. So, I told Shirley I wasn't interested. She could buzz off. You know: scram, get lost, and find herself another sucker. No pun meant or intended. Shirley was mad. If I can use that term to 'spress myself. She was madder than a hatter! Why she stood there callin' me every name in the book and then some I ain't never heard before.

But I didn't care. I calmly told her that she had caught me too late. She don't have no strings on me and I can drop my seed wherever I pleases. Even, if it is a little too late for it to bear fruit. I mean with me past the driving age an' stuff. They don't have no law against driving for people my age. But we cause so many accidents that they should. Old mother f'ers is dangerous. And I'm the first one to admit it. When you hit these numbers you just don't see as good, hear as good or do nothin' else as good. But I'm still getting' my fair share. Anyways like they says: when it's ole to you it's new to somebody else. Ain't it the truth? As y'all can tell by this here letter.

But back to my story.

When I was done upstairs at Shanequa's place I come down to mine and what do I hear as I'm walking down the stairs? On every floor it was the same. That rap crap. Or shit hop or whatever they calls it. Like I said, to each his own. Just cut it down man! Turn it down! I was tired. After all, I done been upstairs with Shaniqua and I was pretty much drained. Pipes sucked out you know and I was in no mood to hear that crap. So, I went down stairs and I called them up on the house intercom. But I guess with the music blastin' they couldn't even hear me. I didn't want to go up to the 4th floor 'cause out of all the 'partments, they the worst offenders. They so bad they leaves one of them speakers in the window. On the window sill. It right next to the fire 'scape and you kin see it when you looks up dere from the coatyard. You kin hear it too!

Man, kin you hear that mother humper! You kin prob'ly hear that sh…playin' halfway 'round the world. And with me only 20 feets away, give or take a few inches, I tell you it's a nightmare. A livin' purgatory that I have to put up wid here. Finally, I gets up enough nerve to call them up from downstairs. I knows it were gonna be trouble and that's why I did it from the innercom. Nobody answered so I rang it again. They ain't been livin' here that long, just three, four years so I figured they didn't know how to work it. Or maybe they forgot how to work the damn thing. You know, people forgits sometimes. I forgits myself. But this time somebody answered. So I said nicely, as nice as I could, "I like your music but I'm tryin' to sleep so could you turn it down a little."

"F..you man," somebody said in the phone, and then they hangs up. Yeah, just like that. I'm not jokin'. I was furious. I was fit to be tied. But I kept my cool. I ain't sh…' you! I took my tired ass all the way up to the 4th floor and rang the bell. They didn't answer so I knocked. Just once or twice. And not loud-loud. It took him a long time to answer but when he comes to the door he was singing that sh…. I guess he must'a thought I was one of his boys.

But when he seen me he stared down at me. I had to look up at him and I s'ppose this gave him courage. "What the f… you want O.G.," he asked?

"She don't live here." "She been dead for years. Just like yo' ole ass." And then he started laughing. I could see one or two of his friends had come in the hallway right behind him and theys laughing too when he said that. Now, I was gittin' madder by the second and I guess I said something I should not have said. I looked him straight in his face and I said. "If you don't turn that damn music down, I'll show you she DOES still live here, 'cause you gonna be my bitch!"

Man, all hell broke loose when I done said dat. He opened up his door and got in my face. He was standing on his toes and sticking out his chest and thumping it like he was the only rooster in a crowded barnyard. But I wasn't 'bout to back down. I could hear the doors of the other tenants on the floor openin' up jest fer 'nough to peek out and still stay out of harm's way. I guess they'd been listenin' on the lower floors too 'cause I would hear about it many times after all the commotion we done made on that day.

I don't have to tell y'all that he couldn't turn the music down now 'cause of his bruised manhood 'n all. But I turned 'round and went back downstairs to my room and closed the door. I think I listened to that rap sh… that night until 5 or 6 in the morning. And the next night too. Why sho it got to me but I'm smarter than that. But I sure wasn't gonna let 'em know it. Whenever we passed on the stoop or in the street I kept right on sayin, 'hello and morning. Whatever was the 'propriate thing to say just like I always done before. I was still a gentlemen. I'm from the old school. I still tips my hat to the ladies and to anybody I figure to be over 40 years or older. They can laugh and call me southern all they wants to but I've never been back down south since we done moved up to New York when I was no more'n 10 years old myself. Lessen they wants to call the South Ferry down south and if I'm not mistaken you go there when you wanna take the boat to Staten Island.

I just wanted to let you know this so that when y'all get this tape and listen to it y'all will understand why I did what I did. I jest 'bout bent over backwards to get along with the folks in dis building. 'specially the young ones. The old folks don't need no special 'tention. They just 'bout understands what they got to do to get along in this here society called The United States of 'Merica. It's the young ones who figure the world OWES dem something. Well, if it does I ain't included in the bill. No buddy, not me. Not Taylor up on dis floor. I done paid my dues and then some. Why some of these young mens and the womenses too. Naw, don't forget the females 'cause they jest as bad. They struts 'round like they got a stick up their behinds. You ever noticed that?

They makes you walk 'ROUND them on the sidewalk. They reaches over you on the buses and trains.

Why they comes right up to you and DEMANDS money and cigarettes like they got a license to.

I'm just not going to tolerate that kind of sh..! After all, I ain't lived to be 'proaching 75 years of age to' be 'timidated by these impolite a..holes. And the FOREIGNERS! Man I don't even know where to start with dem peoples! They cuts in line in front of you and acts like they don't even know you there.

It was better in the forties fitties when I was growing up and we only had to worry 'bout the white man. At least we knew what color we had to watch out for. Nowadays, them peoples who LOOK like us sure ain't our peoples. Now I don't know where they comes from but they ain't no United States of America peoples. They don't know us and they don't like us and I sure as hell don't give a damn about nobody who wants to talk all loud just because we don't understand what they sayin'.

Now I done told you that I ain't prej'dised and I means it. I swears I do but how would YOU like it if somebody got in front of YOU at the supermarket or wherever there was a line formin' and then they just spected you to stand there and give them your spot without saying a word of protest? I'll tell you how you'd like it. You WOULDN'T like it a bit. But dats what they do them peoples and then they just looks at you like you wasn't even standing there. Man, I tell you. I don't know what this place is comin' to. I liked it better before they started letting' all them peoples in the country to take jobs and apartments away from us. That's why I didn't have no use for President Jimmy Carter. He the one that started all that immigration sh... But I'm not gonna bore you with my sad stories.

Let's get to the point of this here 'scussion. Like I done told you. The problem is I can't seem to get no kind of peace around here in my own 'partment. At least it USED to be mine and I still pays the rent and keeps the lights and TV's on and sech. But I sure as hell don't …sider it mine. Not since my wife Rose started letting' all dem kids come back home. Now we ain't got but three bedrooms, a dining room and living room. Which is plenty space for me and the wife but Billy done got sick and done lost his place. His brother (my youngest son) never left home after he got back from the Gulf War and now Rosetta, one of the twin girls left her ol' man and done come back home with a twelve year old girl of her own. Now that makes six of us cramped up in dis little 'partment meant for two. And we only got one bathroom!

I'm just 'bout sick of it. Me and the wife don't get along too much no more 'cause she claim she ain't sexually active no more. She says her body don't produce enough natural lubrication and I hurts her. I don't give a sh.. if hersn don't get wet no more! Mines sure as hell still gets wet and hard too and I'm gonna break it off in something'. She better believe that. It ain't no problem though, not with all the females walkin' round this area. I don't have to go far. It does however present a bit of a problem right here within my home surroundings. That's why I didn't let nobody have the back room back there. I lets the young one and her mother sleep in dere with Rose and the brothers take the bunk beds in the middle room and that's okay with me.

But I keeps the back room for myself. Yes I does. I needs my peace and quiet now and then. And it keeps down the tension 'tween me and the wife a little bit. I really was 'pecting everything to work out just fine and it did. That is 'til the rap music started.

Here's how it goes. We lives in the 2nd floor rear apartment. The people underneath and to the side of us have the little kids like I done already described. Shanequa lives on the third floor and she's not no problem. Oh no, I got no problem with that arrangement whatsoever. And then there's that clown up on the fourth floor. Now that makes three houses in the building on the west side with loud music playing five- six nights a week and half the day. But dere's more to it than that. The building 'rectly to the north I think I got my direction right. Although it's hard to keep your bearings looking at it from this here perspective. The building on the north is another problem. They have a mixed race couple of guys sharing the 'partment on the 3rd floor and a Spanish family on the 1st floor and they all seem to be tryin' to outplay each other in terms of loudness. If I had a had any idea what I was in for when I took this room back here I'd a NEVER done it But you can't blame me with the wife actin' up and all. I mean givin' me those lame excuses just 'cause I want a little piece on occasion.

Well, here's what I done about it. After the argument with the young thug on the 4th floor I figured I had to make amends. You know, bury the hatchet. After all you can't live in a place like this not bein' neighborly. and I just ain't the type to walk around with a chip on my shoulder. So, I went over to 125th Street and I bought the latest rap CD I could find. I come home and walked up to the 4th floor where I rang his bell. When he came to the door he acted like he wanted to shut it in my face but I been selling cigarettes out of my place for a little while now and I had one in my hand which I held out to him. It was a Newport of course and everybody know how we love to smoke Newports. Well, he smiled and took the peace offering just like I know he would and I said to him that I had bought this CD for my 12 year old granddaughter but she already had it and I was wonderin', if he had it. "No," he said. He didn't have it yet. Though he was meanin' to cop one just as soon as he could.

He said he was grateful to me for givin' it to him. Especially after the argument we had and all. But I told him it was no problem for me and we shook hands and that was how the cookie crumbled, so to speak. He said in a kind 'a jokin' way that he wasn't gonna play it too loud and I left and went back downstairs. One out of the way. For the two families underneath me I took a more personal 'proach. I waited 'til the third week of the month when I knows for sure everybody would be runnin' low on food. Food stamps woulda been used up by then and nobody wasn't getting' no more 'til the 2nd or 3rd. I had my daughter clean out that big closet in my kitchen where I keeps a lot of can goods. Or, where I used to keep stuff 'fore they all poured in on me and the wife like it was a rainy day. I figured I could always get more when I gits my pension check on the 1st and Rose gits her stamps. Anyways, I put all dem ol' cans and some sugar and flour too in a couple of big shopping bags and I dropped 'em off at both 'partments. I 'splained that we just got too much food in our house and we couldn't use it all up in month of Sundays.

Now that was the biggest lie I EVER told.

Them knuckleheads in here will eat you out of a house and home if you lets 'em. Noo I ain't lyin'. They eats from the time they wakes up in the morning 'til the time they closes they eyes at night. And I ain't never seen nobody even ACT like the want to do no work. Outsizn 'a working them jaws and elbows.

But that's another story and I don't have no space here to tell it to you 'cause this is only a 90 minute cassette tape as I understands it.

But back to where I was fore I got sidetracked. Them two families were so happy to get them can goods and stuff that I thought they was goin' to smother me with thank yous. I backed out of there and come on home thinkin' that at last I could 'spect to get some respect. After all,

I went outta my way to be neighborly-like. Well, didn't I? Now I know there weren't nothing I could do 'bout the building next door. Beings that I ain't gay. Not that I holds it against them. But I'm just usin' that expression to let you know what MY preferences is. And what was I supposed to give them? A couple of pairs of jock straps?

And as far as the other people go, there ain't no way I 'peaks 'panish. "Ha, ha, I knew that'd put a smile on your face. No, I always wished I could speak another tongue. French, Spanish, I wouldn't give a damn what it was just as long as it was something' some of these other Negroes can't understand. I don't mean to put my people down and I NEVER use that other term term 'cause it ain't respectful. Anyways now we done became African-Americans. Why I 'member the time when that 'N' word could get you kilt. Sho 'nough. I'm not kiddin'. Shot or stabbed to death for calling somebody that word. Now the young folk's: black, white, Spanish, they all uses it like they's just saying good morning! Am I lyin'? Am I lyin? You know I'm telling you the truth!. The things peoples says and does today would make a blind man blush and turn his head in shame.

You know what I 'tended to mention to you while wese on da subject? It's the things that them young GIRLS say. I heared a young girl, couldn't have been no more that 13-14- she told a boy just about her age to suck HER johnson! Can you 'magine that? I sat there on the train shaking my head. WHAT johnson? I said it to myself. I jest don't know no more. I just don't know.

Well, now. My peace offering done I goes home and sat back preparing to get me some much needed rest. I was 'specting to after All I done put myself through and my daughter too. I mean helping me clean out the pantry an' all.

But dem knuckleheads didn't even wait 'til I get in the door 'fore they started that crap. Yakety, Yakety, Yakety, Yak! Then again: Yakety, Yakety, Yakety, Yak! On and on and on and on. I don't know how the hell they understand what dey is sayin'. I sure can't make no sense out of it. And I don't know nobody over 50 who can. All I hear is them cussin' and saying dirty words and making everything rhyme just like they was still in kiddiegarden or something. You think they'd come up with something else sometimes. The artises of my time sang about everything.

It wasn't always about love or hate. Why, I could name you a dozen songs that talk about other stuff 'sides gettin' it on all the time. And that's just me, what I know off the top of my head! Well, I got no rest that night and I don't think I done had a good night's rest since. I was kinda glad I didn't bother with the peoples in the other building next door because I ain't got that kinda money to be throwin' away.

I don't know what they figured I was doin' givin' gifts and my hard earned money away but it look like I done failed in my mission. It look like they didn't get it the e-mail. I mighta done better just throwin' it away or flushin' it down the toilet for all the good it done done! Shucks, I could've spent that money on a piece of Shirley's big you know what. And I wish I had now I think about it.

But I weren't done yet. Not by a long shot. Even at my age I still got a few tricks up my sleeve. An' I was 'bout to put one more in action, baby. And this time I would put my best foot forward. So here's what I did.

Now I had heared the young man say 'fore yesterday that a group of them was planning' on goin' down to Times Square to help the world ring in the New Year. You know. Watch the ball drop and all that Happy New Yearses stuff. You know they always does that every other year or so and then dey comes back home and party and play music for the next 72 hours like they is competin' for a job as a DJ somewhere. It gets hot in these 'partment units, especially in the winter and the Super, he sends up heat like he don't have good sense.

I guess it 'cause he's from some island, I think Dominican Republic and they don't have winter down there I hear. I s'ppose he thinks everybody can take the heat like him. 'cause he sure can't take no cold. You think he'd know by now that this here buildin' don't have no thermostats in the 'partments. It gits so hot up in here sometimes I have to open all the windows in the place. 'Specially in my room. But, the wife she's so scared 'cause y'all still ain't caught that rapist. You know the one I'm talkin' 'bout don't you. The one who goes around climbing in womenses windows and things. He done raped about six, seven females of all ages like that. And the last time he crawled in some broad's BATHROOM

79

window. And get this: he did it from the FIRE ESCAPE. That's where I got the idea I got from.

I figured out I would wait until they all went down to 42nd Street and then I'd go up to the roof, use the fire escape to climb down to the window that they always leaves open. The one with dem speaker that's got to be sitting right next to it. As a matter of fact I know it is because I wouldn't even need to be doin' this otherwise. I seen it there myself, well they put it in the window just last summer during the block party. Everybody had speakers in the windows. Tryin' to outdo everybody else with their own kind of music. It was nightmare in the ghetto time. My youngest come home for the day and when I come upstairs he had MY speakerses sitti'n up in the window getting' ready to blast off. Well, I told that boy, he ain't really no boy at 44 years old but I still calls him that. And hell Rose, that's my wife, says I treats him like a teenager too. I guesses I do some time. But anyways, I give him a piece of my mind right there!

Anyhow, I figures the speakers got to be sitting on the floor or a table near that damned open window. Now all I'm gonna have to do is put one leg over the top rail and into the window and make sure my foot touches the floor inside the apartment. Course I'll be holding on to the rail outside on the fire escape all the time. I'm not STUPID. Do I look stupid? Oh, I forgot, you can't see me, can you? Well, I can tell you that I got all my facilities. Now, once I get my foot over I can reach an' grab inside the window. After that it's gonna be easy to pull myself safe 'cross to the other side and do my work on them speakers. I ain't gonna touch the stereo system. I'm not tryin' to cost nobody no whole bunch a money or nothin'. I just wanna put the speakers outta commission so they won't play so loud and I can get some sleep for at least one night and maybe the next couple of nights too.

I know the other people's gonna be playin' their sh…but I can deal with that a little bit. Least I thinks I can. It mostly that damn

RAP and HIPSTER or HIP HOP that HE be playin'. That's the problem! You knows what I means? And it ain't gonna take but a few seconds to do this. I don't wanna get caught up in no other man's apartment. I ain't getting' shot or stabbed all up. And far as the little distance I need to go from the fire escape to the window? That's a piece of cake. I seen it done many times. In fact I did it once for Shanequa. You 'member I done tol' you 'bout Shanequa, so I don't have to tell you 'bout her no more. Anyways when she got locked out that time and nobody could find the Super. I think he was away sunning himself under pineapple trees or something.

They makes gooood money them supers. Now once I finished my work inside the 'partment cutting the wires or rippin' them out, I don't know what I'm gonna do jest yet. It 'pends on what I see I can do and how them speakers is made. I just want to fix it so it won't amptify the sound no more. You know what I mean. Make it so loud. Least not for a few hours or a couple days. Meanwhile, I can rest and maybe by then figure out how I can give him some money on the sly. Just so he won't 'spect that I'm paying for the damages I know I done caused. I hate to see him pay for my peace and quiet. Young fellow ain't got no job or nuttin'.

As I say, once I complete my work I'll go back out the same way I come in. And just to make it look good I'll leave the window like I done found it. That way he won't even think somebody come in that way.

Now the only other problem I got is telling' the wife Rose that I ain't goin' to see no damn ball drop. I don't care if it IS supposed to be pretty good weather. You can never tell 'bout those things anyways. Them TV weathermen's don't know what the heck they talk' 'bout no how. Why I 'member back in the 60's we went down one New Years to see the ball drop and it turned so cold I just 'bout froze right where I was standing. An' there's all that pushin' and shoving' and mens feeling up on the womenses and stuff.

Maybe the wife gets off like that and I sure as hell don't care. Long as I gets mines. But what I'm talkin' bout here is you gotta hold on to your wallets and pockabooks real tight like 'cause them criminals is everywhere. And the cops ain't gonna protect nobody. Oh, I forgot who I was talkin' to for a minute. Don't pay me no min' 'cause I'm old. That's my plan and I think it's a pretty good one too. I knows you might not agree with me with you bein' cops yourself an' all. But I go to get some peace an' quiet somehow. I done tried everything else.

And with that last thought Benjamin Polk Taylor put the cassette machine on pause and went to relieve himself in the bathroom. He was having an incontinence problem of late and he had intended to have it checked out. In fact, he had scheduled an appointment with his doctor. Even though he didn't particularly like seeing a lady doctor. He felt uncomfortable when she asked him to take his clothes off and kind of embarrassed that he was not the man he used to be. In a few minutes he had returned to his chair with a glass of vodka and soda. He had intended to stop at Shanequa's place just to have a New Year's drink together. Sort of for old times' sake. Then if something else happened it just happened. He was one to just let nature take its course, as he often put it.

Benjamin Polk pushed the pause button and listened as it clicked indicating that the tape was running again. Then he cleared his throat and began speaking in the direction of the built in microphone.

"Ahem, like I was saying," he began again. "Before I rudely interrupted myself by going to relieve my Johnson! I done done just about everything I can do to 'spress myself to these people and I had hoped that they would be willing to c'operate with me an' bend jest a little bit. After all I wasn't asking to do much. Just turn the damn music down a little bit. Cut out the racket. Just Cut The Rap. I don't want to cause nobody no trouble. 'Specially in these troublin' times as it is. I hear tell some is 'pecting this world to end in a couple of years. Twenty-twelve I believe they says.

At least that's what them ole Indian papers and calendars done said. If you can put any trust in somebody's ol' books or whatever it was dey used back then. I didn't even know them peoples could read and write. Least not until right here recent. But lest get back to my explantation. I was just about ready to give up on the whole idea I put in my head to do when the wife come to me three-four days ago and told me that I had to do something about the noise. If I didn't, she was goin'to go to the rent office and 'sist on movin to another building.

I near 'bout lost the little bit of hair I got left on top of my head when she said that! The first thing I thought 'bout was that Shanequa. Well, not 'exactly Shanequa herself but what she carrying 'tween her legs. I knew right away that I had to spring into action. Now the wife took me in her bedroom and told me to sit down. She said, "Shut up and listen." I knew she was real serious then. I didn't have to sit dere long. Maybe 'bout three, four minutes when I heard it. I felt it too. The vibrations I means.

It seems that somebody on t'other side of the wall was playing their music too. Now, the bedroom is sit'ated on the north side of the building if I got my 'rections right this time. My wife's bedroom walls was act'lly shakin'! I could feel it in my knee too. The one I done had that operation on that was givin' me all that trouble two years ago. And it was shakin' all 'cause of them damn woofers an' amtifyin' an' all that bass an' drum sound. I know it had to be Jeffrey. He Ms. Robertses boy. He 'bout twenty or twenty-two years old and she musta bought him a new system for Christmas.

I knew she couldn't a been nowheres in the 'partment 'cause if she was she'd a run him out of dere. Then, I 'member that she is prac'ly deaf in one ear. And she don't have no hearing aid 'cause them peoples at the Medicaid office told her they can't pay for nobody's hearing problems.

And I know for a fact that that's true 'cause I got another friend who done told me jest 'bout the same thing. I figure no wonder the boy playing that damn Rap so loud! I told Rose I'd do somethin' 'bout it and that just what I'm planning' to do tonight.

I'm just about through telling' you what I go to tell you on this here tape recorder. Bought it a few years ago in a sale on 125th and Lenox and it still work. Yeah, it was a good deal. It still work just fine. But like I said, I'm not goin' to make myself a pest or bore you or nothing' like that but I just wanted to clear up something' I told you back a little piece. Now I done 'splained about the cigarettes I been sellin' and the reason for my sellin' 'em. Mostly, just to have somethin' to do and to have something' to say to my neighbors. Bein' that I ain't got no work to go to no more. But I stopped sellin' them cigarettes to folks a week 'fore Christmas. I may have sold a couple more on Christmas Day when most of the stores 'round here was closed early. Even those A- rab stores. They closed early Christmas Day and some was closed up tight as a drum all day long. I was surprised by that. But since then, I ain't sold not one. No, sir! I tell folkses I'm out of business.

Gon' fishin'! Some of 'em gets mad and says I'm lyin' but I don't care. Rose told me I never should have started sellin' those damn loosies and I 'spect she's right. Now I just wanted to make that clear to you.

Case you was plannin' to come round here and 'rest me for breakin' some law I don't know nothing 'bout. And the last thing I wanna do here is "pologise for some of the cussin' and the bad words I been doin'. I kind a got away with myself. With the wife not here to put a controlling' hand on me. If you understands what I means.

I ain't tryin' to claim to be no church goin' Christian but I AM a Christian. Was raised that away. And I sure as hell don't do much cussin'. Less I'm with the mens folks; the few ones that left that is. Most of 'em done left this earth a long time ago. Them that didn't get kilt died from drugs and cigarette smokin'. Though a few died most recently from AIDs. That's a BAD ASS thing and Rose said it's a wonder I ain't dead from it, spreading my seed all over the place. She 'zagerates sometime Rose does but she might got a point. Though she don't know it. Lessen I'd be dead already from domestic abuse. Well, that's about it. I hope I'm not gonna have to produce this tape in a court of law or nothing like that. But just in case, I'm puttin' it in a closed envelope and leavin' it right here on my night stand.

I done wrote across the top: FOR THE COPS IN CASE I GETS 'RESTED. Just in case I gets 'rested or something. I sure don't wanna spend no time on Rikers Island 'cause I done heard it's a nasty place to go. And they got all those young bucks out there wildin out and shit. 'scuse me! I means stuff! But I been DRIVEN to do this, as you can see. And Rose, that's my wife as y'all knows by now, can be my witness and testify in court to that part.

Signin' off now, Benjamin Polk Taylor, 2330 Morningside Avenue, New York City on December 31st, 19... I means 2009 nine at 10:47 P.M. See, I told y'all I'm old. I even thinks old!

Benjamin P. Taylor, stood up from his chair and took a long drink from his glass. He was satisfied with his work and he was tired. He had a lot to do and he knew that with the clock ticking he had but one hour to do it. He didn't have much time before the young man and his friends would be returning from Times Square. They would be high and ready to make life miserable for him with their Rap CD's and they would be blasting them all morning long from the 4th floor window near the fire escape. He wanted to prevent this torture, then have that drink with Shanequa and be home with his wife. Of course he wouldn't be there at midnight to see the ball drop but at least he'd be there to shut her mouth.

He changed into all black attire and his black high top sneakers.

He remarked to himself that he cut a handsome figure still. Then, straightening the collar of his black turtle neck sweater he smoothed his pants and noted his still flat stomach. He hated to see anyone his age wearing fitted clothes while sporting a pot belly- especially mens folks as he called them. Although the sneakers were not Jordan's he remarked that they looked good on his feet. He smiled when he remembered that he'd bought them with a white pair at a two for one sale near Chambers Street during the summer. He had paid thirty-nine dollars for both pairs.

Just before he walked out he poked his head into the living room and mumbled to his wife Rose that he was going to the lobby to see if there were any of the friends they both knew passing through. He would talk with them for a minute and offer them a little taste of his good cheer. He showed her his bottle and patted it for good measure. Rose hardly looked at him. She reacted with her usual disinterested "umm hmmm" and continued watching the performers at the Times Square show. She seemed bored as she switched channels. When he was almost through the door he realized he'd forgotten to put a pair of scissors in his pocket along with the wire cutters and he went back inside.

"Forgot something, Bill Cosby?" "What you mean Bill Cosby," he asked? "Well, you goin' out dressed up like him from I SPY so I thought I'd call you by his name," she replied. "Oh, you got jokes, Moms." His was a reference to the comedienne Moms Mabley and an acknowledgement that he had noticed how his wife was dressed. She caught the hint and laughed. "HAPPY NEW YEAR," she yelled! He let the door close hard.

Once outside the door he quickly put his plan into action. He knew he was taking an awful risk by doing things this way but he had no other choice. If he succeeded in his efforts it was going to make things better for a whole lot of other folks who wished they'd had the nerve to do it. Quiet as it was kept. Anyway, this was the last holiday party and as bad as things were on regular weekdays, mornings and weekends, they weren't likely to get any worse for a few days more. At least not until the next holiday in two weeks or so.

He was thinking of the Martin Luther King Jr. bash someone upstairs always threw on the man's birthday. Benjamin Polk thought about the insult to the memory of the man and shook his head.

Why the man must be turning over in his grave, he thought with genuine sadness. He also thought of what the great one would think of what he, Benjamin Taylor was up to now and the thought almost made him lose his nerve. But he regained his composure and determination once he remembered that between now and January 15th there was sure to be somebody's birthday party or two or three somebody's.

Then there was February. February had Valentine's Day and the weekend with President's Day. A whole bunch of folks came into this world in February he remembered. This included his own Rose and his twelve year old granddaughter. She'll be thirteen, he recalled. Slowly he climbed the stairs to the last landing. When he got to the fourth floor he paused for more than a few minutes to listen. To make sure he didn't hear sounds coming from apartment 41 - C. He convinced himself that it was the reason he had stopped for such a long minute. Benjamin did not want to admit that he was totally out of breath. One more short flight he told himself and then I'll be out of view and out the door.

Feeling a chill he realized that some idiot had left the landing door half open. That's why us poor folks can't get nowhere, he thought. We always ruinin' other people's businesses. Then, noticing the cigarette butts, ashes and a couple of old condoms in the corner, he rolled his eyes in distaste. "No class," he said out loud.

Once out on the roof he walked in the direction of the west side of the building. For a second he lost his sense of direction he took another look before he could identify a few of the area's land marks.

Satisfied, he got down on his knees and crawled slowly toward the edge of the roof.

It was then that he realized that there was something missing. There was no fire escape leading to the roof. There was only a ladder with very thin rungs. It looked unsafe. He gripped it and pulled to test it.

The thing seemed secure enough and he tugged hard to be certain it was strong enough to hold him. He was sure it would not have been there if it was dangerous. After all there were laws against unsafe fire escape he recalled. It was a long way down to the yard below and just one slip, one false move and he would be scrambled eggs. But ALL the old buildings HAD to have a fire escape if they were more than four or 5 stories tall. Even the school he worked at downtown after his retirement from the Transit Authority had a full fire escape and it was eight stories.

Including the roof.

How could he have made THAT mistake? Again he looked over the edge of the roof.

It wasn't more than eight or nine feet to the fourth floor fire escape. If he had a rope and some way to secure it he could lower himself down easy. He could climb back up the same way to make his escape. And there was plenty light from the courtyard below to see what he was doing so that part wouldn't be dangerous.

Suddenly, Benjamin remembered the rope he had bought when he had his old pickup truck and was doing light moving jobs in the neighborhood. He'd never made much money and after a year or so he had thrown in the towel. The rope was still there and in the closet just as you walked in the door of his apartment. That would do just fine if he could sneak it out of the house past Rose.

He took his time and walked back down the stairs. He made certain that he was not overheard. Entering his apartment he could hear the television from the living room and he walked toward it.

He was prepared to tell his wife the lie he'd invented on the way down but when he got there he found her fast asleep. He retraced his steps and slowly opened the closet door. As he'd hoped the rope was pushed to the rear of the closet. It was full of dust. In an instant he had it under his arm and was walking out the door.

He retraced his steps to the roof where he slipped a short length of the rope through the back edge of the door and pulled it around enough to make a slip knot. That done Benjamin now fastened the loop to the inside door knob and pulled it as tight as possible. He knew the clock was ticking and he worked fast. For greater security he repeated the process and within a few minutes he was done. Finally, he closed the door on the rope.

Taking the rope in his hand he inched toward the fire escape and dropped the rope over the edge of the roof. It just barely reached the steps of the fire escape and Benjamin smiled with relief. But he knew it would be fool hearty to just hang himself over the edge of the roof without tying the rope around his waist a couple of times. He quickly pulled the rope to the roof where he tied himself tightly. He even did it twice for good measure and then just to be certain he doubled checked it. After all, he thought. I'm not tryin' to hang myself tonight!

But Benjamin had made a serious error in judgement. By tying the rope around his waist twice he had miscalculated. It would leave him a few feet short of the narrow walkway on the fire escape. And he needed to plant his feet on something solid in order to undo the knots, do his deed and then redo them to pull himself up again once he was finished his work. But he didn't realize his error until he'd lowered his body over the edge of the roof and was halfway down the short ladder between the roof and the fire escape.

He noticed that his body had come to a sudden halt and to untie himself at that point would have left him dangling and swinging like a performer in a circus trapeze act. Of course he knew he could have clung to the short ladder but he didn't feel it was safe enough. Almost panicking he used all his strength to untie the knots. Sweating bullets and trying hard not to look down he worked feverishly.

Somewhere he'd heard that the first law for people who worked from heights was: never look down! At least that's what he remembered being told by a friend who had done that kind of work. Of course he was long dead.

Benjamin Polk Taylor did not look down. He let his body drop the four feet to the metal walkway of the fire escape. But in his haste he had made another miscalculation. He had not noticed that the walkway on the fire escape was only about twenty inches wide. There was an opening on the other side of the walkway another foot and a half wide. And the opening was wide enough for a thin man such as himself to fall through. Fall through all the way to the ground!

But he didn't fall to the ground this New Year's Eve. He only fell half through the opening. He skinned his shins and his arms in the process and bruised his body. He scared himself half to death in the process.

By the time he recovered and got a hold of himself another ten minutes had passed and when he looked at his watch it read 11:43 P.M. Seventeen minutes to midnight. He thought about that drink with Shanequa. It wasn't going to happen tonight he was sure of that much.

From the fire escape the speakers in the window in apartment 41-C looked far away.

And the ground four stories down looked that way too. He knew he wasn't going to be able to follow through with his original plans. Benjamin would have to be creative. He thought that if he leaned over far enough his fingertips could touch the speaker closest to him. He would try to pull it in his direction. Just far enough to 'do something' to it.

To do anything that would damage it and shut it up for just one night, one day, one hour.

He hadn't come this far and nearly killed himself for nothing. He stretched out his arms and stood on his toes, holding fast to the rail of the fire escape. Even putting his right foot and knee through the opening to give himself more support and balance in case of another mishap. But the speaker was still too far away. He needed another three or four inched to pull it toward him. He needed ... ... the scissors! Yes, that would do it!

Quickly, he pulled the scissors from his back pocket and used them to maneuver the heavy speaker slowly in his direction. This took another few minutes of straining and trying again and again until at last. At last the speaker was close enough to grab. Putting the scissors in his pocket once more he took out the screw driver he had brought along and the wire cutters. He was nearly ready to cut the wire when he heard something crash. The other speaker had fallen heavily to the floor inside the apartment.

"OH SHIT!" Benjamin said. He nearly said excuse my French but he knew that would have been dumb. Not a soul was listening. Well, now they'll think a burglar was tryin' to steal the damned thing and that ain't the worse thing in the world they can think, he thought. He went back to his work of disabling the speaker and cutting the remaining ties with the one now on the floor inside the room.

When he had completed his handiwork he put the screw driver away and was straining to put it back in its place inside the window when disaster struck again. The speaker fell from the window. But this one did not fall inside. It did not fall to the floor of the apartment as the other speaker had done. It fell from the window ledge to the outside of the metal guard rail and went down. All the way to the cemented court yard below. And it did so at the stroke of midnight. Just as the people in the area and in Times Square and in hundreds of thousands of places across the city were screaming and celebrating. Just as car horns were blowing, people were shouting Happy New Year and "Auld Lang Syne" was being sung.

The thing fell into the courtyard below and nobody paid it any attention. They thought it was a part of someone's festivities. With his nerves a wreck and his mind racing, he tried to decide on his next course of action. For certain he needed t get off that damned fire escape and he needed to get down safely. There was only one thing he could do. He would have to go down the fire escape and take the chance of getting caught climbing into his own window. That would be in the wife's bedroom and he wasn't even sure she had left the window open just a little as he told her she should do.

Well, he had to try, he had to! Slowly he descended the cold metal monster. The weather had turned bitterly cold just as he had suspected it might and he knew he had to get off that thing and back up to the roof to collect the rope before the young man came home and discovered the damages to his apartment, He'd call the police and then all hell would break loose. He knew he'd be in a mess of trouble.

Down he went until he reached the window of his wife's bedroom but it was closed and the blinds and curtains were drawn.

"Damn you Rose," he said. He blew his breath into his hands to warm them. He looking up on the side of the building but he couldn't see a light. He blinked and look again. There appeared to be a light on in the bathroom window of 31-C. It was the apartment of Virginia Hudson. And that bitch don't like me, he said to himself. Well, I'll have to take my chances and tell her I got locked out. Say I heard something fall and come out on the fire escape to investigate.

Say I saw a burgular come down the fire stairs and I was trying to follow him but he got away. Nobody don't know that rope belongs to me 'cept Rose an' she my wife and they can't force her to testify against me. 'Course I'll have some 'splainin' to do with her too. He had it all worked out in his mind as he reached in his pocket and took another drink.

HAPPY NEW YEAR, he almost shouted. But in his mind he added another two words: old fool!

Benjamin walked back to the third floor fire escape landing and reached over to the bathroom. The window was open about six inches and the light was being turned off as he tapped on the window. Desperate to get someone's attention he leaned and tapped hard. Remembering the fall of the speaker and how hard it had hit the ground he looked down.

Inside the apartment sixty-six year-old Virginia Hudson had just finished brushing her teeth as she did every night before retiring. It was the fourth time that day she had done so and she was satisfied. She prided herself that at her age she still had all her teeth except the wisdom teeth and the one she had lost in a freak bicycle accident. But it had been replaced. The dentist had done a good job. Virginia lived alone now that her husband was dead and she wasn't too unhappy about that. She had become used to being alone. But she had been nervous since the recent rash of rape events in the neighborhood.

When she heard the rap on the window she quickly closed the bathroom door but she stood just outside.

She didn't move and she knew she had to. The window was open a bit. It had been foolish of her. Given the times and the circumstances. Slowly, she opened the door and looked in. She knew she had to close the window at all costs. Horrified, she watched as a man stuck his head inside and called her name. "Ms. Hudson, Ms. Hudson!" She quickly walked over to the window without turning on the light and to Benjamin Taylor's amazement Ms. Hudson brought the window down on his fingers as hard as she could. He screamed as loud as he could.

But Virginia Hudson wasn't listening. She hurried to the telephone and dialed 911. "I caught him," she said calmly.

"I, Virginia Hudson just caught the rapist you have been looking for and you'd better get right over here." She gave her address and telephone number.

Meanwhile, Rose Taylor apartment 21 -C had woke up too late to see the ball drop in Times Square. She hadn't woke up on her own. Something had woke her. It sounded like somebody had thrown something heavy out of an upstairs window and she hoped they were not beginning again to toss the garbage out of the windows. They'd done that when another family lived in 41-C.

At first she was angry that her husband had not come in to make sure she didn't miss the ball drop at midnight. After all they were both getting old and who knew how many more times they would live to see that happen. Particularly together. Death didn't frighten her. She started to go to the kitchen to begin warming up the late meal she knew everyone would want when they came in from the parties and places they all had gone to. She supposed that a few might have gone down to 42nd Street. But she didn't care, she told herself. She had no intentions of participating in that kind of foolishness. It was cold out there. She had prepared a nice midnight meal.

This was a once a year tradition but this year there wouldn't be tons of food. It wasn't a pig fest. Nobody had to over -eat she reasoned.

Passing the room her husband now called his lounge she looked in to call him to his New Year's meal. But he wasn't there. A quick search of the house revealed that he wasn't in the apartment. Rose began to worry. She had heard him talking to someone in his room earlier and at times he sounded agitated. Maybe there was something wrong. Maybe, he had come back, got his warm coat and then gone to meet a woman! She would check to see if his coat was still there on the chair. Rose Thigby Taylor, wife of Benjamin Polk Taylor walked back to the small room her husband used for his hideaway and the first thing she saw was his coat thrown over the chair as was always his habit to do. She was ready to close the door when she noticed something she had not seen in a long time. There on the table was the old cassette recorder he was so much in love with a few years back.

"Why I wonder what he was doing with that old thing," she asked. Then she saw the envelope. She picked it up, noticed it was sealed and marked to the attention of the Police department. "Oh my God." She screamed! "The poor man's done gone home to Jesus!"

He done committed suicide! That was all that commotion I heard in the courtyard a while back.

Well, I can't look back there, he's probably all broke up and busted, with blood everywhere."

Rose reached for the telephone and dialed 911. "Hello, I'm Rose Taylor, wife of Benjamin Taylor of …

She gave her address and explained that her husband had just committed suicide after leaving a tape recording for the police. She didn't have the courage to open the envelope and listen to it.

Upstairs on the 3rd floor Virginia Hudson stood outside her bathroom door holding a kitchen knife. With the police on their way she listened as the man at the window tried to explain who he was and just what he was doing out there. But she wasn't having any of it. "I know who you are ole Ben Taylor," she said. "You think I don't recognize you after all these years? I knew who you was the moment I seen you out there. And don't you think I was surprised either. I ALWAYS suspected you was involved in those rapes. Struttin' around here with your manhood showing and acting like you still a young buck! Why it's a disgrace. You don't deserve that nice wife of yours. You're a sex fiend and you have always been one. I knew that the minute I laid eyes on you. Don't you go thinking I don't know your kind! I've seen your kind before. I heard tell you been sneaking round here and messin' with that Shanequa upstairs! Oh yes, Benjamin Taylor, everybody in the building's been talking about it! They been talkin' on it for months. Well, now we'll see how smart you are. You, you alley cat! You might have raped them other poor women by sneaking in their bathroom windows but this time you met your match. Oh no, you didn't get to rape this one. If you had just had the common sense to come see me and talk over your problems, none of this would have ever happened. You didn't have to go around raping and carrying on. I'm a single woman now and I can be discreet too. Nobody would ever have known what we were doing.

Virginia was still talking to him this way when the police arrived at Rose Taylor's door. They took the tape in their possession and left someone there to console her while they investigated the claim of her husband's demise. They had still not completed the search for his body when the second group of officers arrived to make their way upstairs to apartment 31-C where Virginia Hudson stood talking to her captive audience. Except this time he didn't have anything to say. And it would have done him no good to try because she wouldn't let him get a word in edgewise. Yakety, Yakety, Yak!

LUF, ME
(NEXT DOOR TO A FRIEND)

"BUT WILT THOU know, O vain man, that faith without works is dead?" - James II - 20 -King James Version

With only eight days left before Christmas Day Maurice had decided to leave the apartment. It was going to be a difficult thing to do. Just moving from a place where he'd lived for forty years was tough. It wasn't just the throwing away of mementoes and the parting of ways of old friends. There were the intangibles. The familiar walls and faces of the building. Even the smells coming from the apartments of other residents as they prepared their nightly meals; the habits of the doormen, the oddities of people as they went about their daily habits. These are the things that somehow get stuck in the brain without notice.

There was no rush to move out. Everything had been worked out with the owners and it was possible to delay the move until the week after Christmas. Just as long as he was out before January 1ˢᵗ. That was all he needed to worry about. But what difference did

one week actually make? It was not going to be any easier to move just before the New Year. He had to go, so he'd just as well move sooner than later. Sever all ties now and have it over and done with. Move on and carry no old baggage and memories. As if that would ever be possible to do with forty years of fond events stuck in one's sub-consciousness.

There were a million things to do. There was not only the packing. There was serious cleaning to do in the old place. Some of his heavier furniture had not been moved in a couple of years. It had been simpler for him to just clean around things. He didn't like cleaning the apartment. Especially after he'd gone into the cleaning business. It was enough to have to make a living telling people how to clean. He certainly didn't want to come home and have to do it. And he'd never had to either. His godmother had always taken care of that for him and even after she'd had a stroke and passed he'd had someone come in and do the cleaning. Sadly, the hard economic times of the past four or five years had brought that all to an end.

The good times were gone.

And the recession hit him where it hurt most: in the pocket. It had become difficult enough just to pay the bills and to keep a roof over his head. He'd felt it coming on for at least that long. Most economist and learned minds were reporting that the hard times had happened only in the second half of the current 2008 calendar year but he knew better. Of course, the brunt of it didn't hit until the stock market fell and the insurance companies and banks began failing but he had watched it all as it unfolded affecting his small business.

People simply were not hiring minority companies like his to do the work anymore. They no longer felt the need or the obligation to do affirmative action. Anyone could claim to be a minority and get away with it. In fact, he knew of several cases. The owners of the businesses had been no more a member of a minority than

Jack Sprat was but they had somehow qualified as such. There were so many ways to get around the rules. Once the contracts were awarded there was nothing anyone could do about it. Or, at least nothing anyone chose to do. For all the hoopla that was made over the creation of this farce, help for struggling Black American Businesses was waning and fast. Moreover, no one seemed to give a damn about it. The by word was that discrimination was dead in America. The playing field had been evened and it was wrong to even profess anything else.

Being Black American was not 'in' anymore. At least not as far as getting support for economic elevation was concerned. There were no loans to be had and there seemed to be little or no infrastructure that had been created by Black Americans with the capital to do so. He had tried only once to get help but the paper work was so extensive and exhaustive that he'd soon realized the only way to play the game was to be dishonest. Guye refused to compromise his integrity in that way. And he didn't have to look far to gain support for this decision. Just next door; to his longtime friend and confidant. Integrity and honesty were her by- words and she lived them daily. The end finally came in the third week of March. It was then that he received what he termed as his Dear Guye letter. Guye was not his given name. Very early in the business he'd simply dressed up Guy with an 'e'. His had been a one man office and 'starting up' he had used the name as a kind of second officer in the company. Back then it had been the name he was most known by in the music industry. But that had been a dozen years earlier.

Now, in the new millennium he was financially committed to the cleaning business in New York City. And after many years of service his oldest client called him in and announced that they were moving in a different direction. They'd made a big show of it all. There had been everything except tears from the Director whom

Guye had known and come to admire but in the end it was all made quite clear his company's services would no longer be required after June 30th, 2008.

That was all. He was being replaced by an in house crew that could be easier controlled. Even though it was going to be more expensive to do it that way. They were willing to pay the extra money. It was worth it in the long term: so they said. Actually, he knew it had nothing to do with cutting costs. It was more a case of greed. It also smacked of blatant racism. They wanted to put a whiter face forward. It helped with the annual donations to the school. Now that the African American business manager had retired and was sick with an inoperable cancer there was no one at the school to support him and to appreciate the countless hours of service he had given them. Services that were over and above the call of duty. There was no point complaining about it. It was all water over the bridge and time to move on.

Had this decision been made a couple of years earlier he'd have been more equipped to deal with it but as things go he knew there is never a right time. In retrospect, knowing how things in the world were moving, he had put all his available revenue into trying to shore up loose ends and in rebuilding. It hadn't been enough and the end had come faster than expected. After many years of service he had terminated the last few employees, said goodbye and left with his dignity and honor intact. He'd gone home, practically broke and bloodied but unbowed. He had been brought up to treasure his dignity and honor and it meant more to him than money.

That was an accomplishment he knew. He had stolen from no one, he had begged no one and he owed no business creditors. Most of all he hadn't wasted his time. He knew how to do several other things and there was great hope for the future. Perhaps it would take a few days longer than tomorrow but he would get there with a little help above and from his friends. Not money or influence but moral support. He depended on their moral support. Especially the help of two of them. They were both older women. One black and the other white and they had always been there for him just as he had for them. The only problem was that one was dying and the other elderly. He had hoped to be able to give them help as they aged without his added worry of how to make a good living in a struggling economy.

There were of course others who had stuck by him. He had his family and a few friends and although most of the older people were long deceased there still a whole slew of siblings, nieces and nephews left in the world. Guye preferred not to bother any of them with his troubles. He had always been the one who had helper everyone he could. How could he suddenly reverse gears and ask them for favors? He couldn't do it and he knew he never would. Every tub had to stand on its own bottom was the way his father had put it to all of them and by Jove he was determined to stand on his. Even if it killed him. Besides, there were the children to consider. He had none of his own but there were several godchildren. He was concerned about them. Particularly the younger ones. They had always depended on his generosity and support. Not only financial support but tutoring in homework and extra activities like piano lessons and French lessons or just general knowledge lessons.

They were a fine bunch, from the eldest to the youngest and now a new generation was born. How could he just walk off and leave them to the elements?

Perhaps he was over -stating his importance to them but Guye didn't think so. That's the difference between adults and children, he often said. Children cannot fake emotional ties. Either they trust you and love you or they don't. They haven't yet learnt the art of deception. And that had been proven by the last night in the apartment. He had hoped to leave earlier that day but the movers had taken forever to do their job. They had promised to take no more than 4 hours to empty the apartment.

But they'd taken nearly eleven hours. They'd promised three men to do the packing and moving. Although that had been the case at the beginning, after an hour the third man had left the apartment leaving the other two to complete the job. Of course, there was the time off for breaks and the lunch hour. By the time it was all finished the final cost was three times as much as the estimator had promised. It was all a sham and although he knew he was being had he said nothing. He was already in a sorry emotional state and he didn't need to put himself through the wringer. He paid the bill and asked the building's superintendent for permission to spend the night there.

It was a good thing he was throwing away the old sofa because it was a sleeper and the extra night was spent rather uncomfortably wrapped in a warm blanket but in an otherwise empty apartment. The kids had stayed with him as long as they could. At least three of them had remained there until well after 10 p.m. It was difficult enough just to sit and talk with them, reminiscing about the good times in the place while being uncertain and apprehensive about the future. It would have been a whole lot easier had there been another place to move to in the city but this was not the case. He'd contacted friends in Albany, New York and they told him of a place there. A small two - bedroom apartment that was right beneath their own. They promised him that he would love the place and since he had nothing else in mind he'd agreed to go there sight unseen. It was a foolish thing to do but he was confident at the time that the friends knew his tastes and his style. He was mistaken.

He knew that the future in Albany would be uncertain: with feeling his way around and learning how to live in a different environment and in an unfamiliar world of strange and casual acquaintances. But there had been no other choice. Now, on the eve of leaving the familiar and the loved, he sat there talking with the kids and by the time they were ready to leave everything that could be discussed had been talked of several times over. It was impossible to avoid the inevitable. The two males, aged 17 and 20 were strong enough to put on brave faces.

But the youngest, a girl of 14 years had fallen apart emotionally and this had a ripple effect on the little group now contemplating saying what appeared to bea final goodbye.

Guye had finally begged them to take her out and away from him. Then, in one uncontrolled burst of emotion he'd shut his bedroom door and given way to his own feelings of frustration and helplessness. But there was hope. There was plenty of hope and he would come to understand that over the next few weeks and months. He would begin to understand that losing his business and his financial base had been perhaps one of the best things that ever happened to him.

But on that last night in the apartment there was one more link to sever. One more goodbye to say and perhaps a few more tears to shed. He had to walk next door, knock on his neighbor's door and say goodbye to his friend of forty years. Her name was Betty and since they'd met she had been his most ardent fan and staunch supporter. That had been a long time ago. Back then he was very young and she was still in early middle age. Although she didn't think so, she'd been almost pretty then. She liked to say that she was as plain as a mud pie but it wasn't so.

She really was an attractive woman and she had been more so in her early years. She had suffered all her life from the scourges of asthma and she had periods where it seemed to drain all her strength. She often said that as a young person she was not expected to live long. But like the story he'd had heard several times from his own grandmother, Betty had survived and would continue living a relatively healthy existence for quite a few years longer. Just as his grandmother had done at the age of three when good medical minds of the times said she wouldn't live to reach five years.

Granny had made it to through at least nine Presidents; to see three Centuries. "Oh Betty, you'll probably outlive me and everyone else in this building," he would tease.

They were an odd couple. There was certainly nothing untoward about their relationship. Just good neighbors and friends in its purest meaning. She had her life and he had his and they seldom discussed their personal relationships. Only once or twice she's asked him for his advice and opinion. He never once told her anything about his personal relationships and if she guessed, she had the good taste not to interfere. It was just as well because his tastes were always changing and evolving and what was in vogue with him last year might not be so the next. Besides, with the large family and the extended family and work experiences they both had over the years there had been plenty to keep them talking for another 50 years.

And the past. There was always the past. Betty had been born in Pittsburgh, Pennsylvania. Guye also had ties in Pittsburgh. Before moving to Chester, Pa. it had been the family seat of his grandmother and grandfather and a host of great aunts and uncles. They had gone there from Macon or Cochran, Georgia sometime in the early '20's or late teens. Some were still there, although he had no idea where. He'd never been to Pittsburgh as his immediate family had settled in the southern part of the State. So there wasn't much to talk about on that score.

Still, it was a good jumping off point and the stories she told of her childhood in that town were both amusing and sometimes sad. She told him not only of her struggles to live with asthma but of a mostly blissful but sometimes turbulent childhood. Of her parent's divorce and the death of a younger brother. She told him of her mother's struggle to survive the hard times of the worst depression the nation had ever known and how they'd had to move from the big beautiful house they had apparently owned and lived in to more modest dwellings. Of a mother who worked as a teacher and did part -time volunteer work to support a growing family and of how it came to be that Betty determined never to be without the basics for survival. Mainly, a good store of food in the pantry and in any closet.

There were many, many more heartwarming and good stories to listen to as the relationship moved from its infancy of feeling each other out to one of mutual kindness and trust. These were also the years of her employment at The Brooklyn Polytechnic Institute. She didn't make much money but she seemed to enjoy most of the time she worked there. Betty often shared stories of her relationships at Polytechnic and when she left there for good the two of them read and re - read her letter of resignation until she had it just right.

In the early years her mother would drive up from Pittsburgh at least twice a year to spend time with her daughter. She always came with a supply of homemade cookies. Cookies of several varieties. She put them in tins and lined the bottoms with waxed paper. It was all so neat and homey and it reminded Guye of the times of his youth when he'd spent looking through the glass doors at the cakes and pies his grandmother Mollie made and stored in her cabinet. They all looked so tasty and tempting and it was one of his fondest memories about the old attached house they'd lived in on West 2nd Street in Chester, Pennsylvania. Maybe there was something to be said about the older women who had lived their lives in that state. It seemed that most of them had learned to cook and sew. At least the few he'd known in his life. But they were a dying breed and he was convinced that now, only Betty's mother, could bake cookies that tasted so good. Even the neighbors or whomever was lucky enough to sample them could attest to that fact.

She was of German heritage and she looked like the wonderful pictures of German housewives Guye had seen portrayed in old magazines and movies. Not in a stereotypical way but in a kind of warm and fuzzy fashion. Naturally, she was anything but an oversimplified picture of herself. She had a very modernistic approach to the problems of the times and she expressed them. The last time xhe'd driven to New York from Pittsburgh that Guye could remember was the year of her eighty-six or eighty -seventh birthday. It was around Christmas time and she stayed until after New Year's Day. The next thing he recalled hearing was that she was leaving her home and moving to New York to live next door with her daughter. After that, the years became a mixed blend of illnesses and growing old as Betty struggled to care for her mother in the apartment and to deal with her own growing and on -going health concerns.

Sadly, in a few short years her mother would die and with her loss all would be a poorer but richer that she'd lived and died there. It would not be until after her mother's passing that Betty would often confess that she'd always felt her mother never loved her. She'd loved her brother the well-known Psychiatrist but she'd paid Betty little more than lip service. There were other things that Betty told him. She said she never felt as if she measured up in her mother's eyes. That she never felt attractive around her or smart enough and that she blamed her mother for breaking her father's will and spirit. Betty was daddy's little girl and when her parents divorced she was still a teen. She said it had nearly destroyed her. Guye remembered one very funny story Betty told him of the divorce. It turned out that it was also one more of his greatest lessons on living.

It seems that it occurred at a time in this country's history when divorce was considered almost as awful as a crime deserving of corporal punishment. Those who had divorced were shunned and very often their children were looked upon with pity and scorn. Like most important local news of the day it had made the newspapers. One of her brothers alerted her to that truth right after breakfast one Saturday morning. "Sis, I want you to be prepared to brave the big bad world outside," was his way of understating the event. But the news had hit the print on a Saturday and Saturdays were the times she met her friends for a ride downtown to Pittsburgh's largest shopping district. There they would have time to browse the stores and window shop and perhaps purchase a few inexpensive items. They would laugh and sometimes go to a movie and end the day with an ice cream cone or soda at a favorite drug store or soda fountain.

Betty thought of reneging on her sworn obligation to accompany her girlfriends but it was no use. She had to put her selfish feelings aside and swallow her pride. She had to meet her friends on the bus at the appointed hour. She felt that almost life itself depended on their Saturdays together. Betty left the house on time and waited for her bus to arrive. But she stood there hoping! Hoping that the friends would not would not be on the bus. That they would have missed it or, having seen the article in the newspapers, they would have already decided that she had lost status and could no longer be a member of their group. That would be the sporting thing to do, she thought. Spare her the looks of false pity and pretense. Forego the snide comments that would only serve to push the knife in further. And finally, the pitying twist of the blade as they looked at her- tongues clucking like hens in a barnyard. But alas, the bus pulled to a halt in front of her. She boarded it and paid her fare.

Already she could see the other girls seated in their usual seats. They had reserved a place for her. The guillotine: the place of her execution. Slowly she walked forward. The last mile Betty thought to herself as she slunk down as low as she could in the seat. Surely, this was what it felt like to be on death's row. To have witnesses waiting in the wings for you to die while they drank warm milk and ate peanut butter and jelly sandwiches. Or sipped tea and ate crumpets. The bus moved on and although she waited no one said anything for quite a spell.

Finally, unable to stand the suspense any longer she sat up straight. Well, if they are not going to be adult enough to get to the point then I will, she said to herself. I'll take the initiative. I'll go on the attack! I will not sit here being silent and defensive about this. Her strength now sufficiently gathered, she looked at her friends and asked indignantly. "Well, has anyone read the newspapers?" They looked from one to the other in puzzlement, lifting their shoulders in a hunch. Betty repeated her question. "Hasn't anyone read today's newspaper," She demanded? After what seemed like an eternity one of the girls said. "Of course we've read the newspapers, don't we always?" "Well, what did you think," Betty asked? She was glad that was at last out in the open.

"Well, there's a sale of hats at Penney's" one of the friends replied. "A of what, where?' Betty answered incredulously. "My parents have divorced, the news is all over Pittsburgh and here you sit talking about a sale of hats at Penney's!" "Oh!" the friends responded almost as one. They looked hopelessly from one to the other. They wondered what the fuss was about. There was silence for a second or two until someone offered her a copy of the newspaper she'd been reading. Pointing to a page she pushed it in front of Betty. "Well, there is a sale she said defiantly!" She'd thought Betty hadn't believed her.

Betty told Guye this story about her past several times and it never failed to crack him up. It was a lesson he would always remember and something he would think of whenever he thought of her.

Never be concerned about what others think. Theirs is rarely an accurate measuring stick.

People are only as concerned as YOU imagine them to be. If they talk about you and they often will, it only lasts for about 15 minutes. After that they are off to another topic.

Betty was one of the only people Guye remembered who had actually attended the famous March on Washington. She took the bus down and participated along with the thousands of others who heard the famous speech, "I Have a Dream." And she was one of the first activists Guye had ever met. She often told him how she'd become a member of the West Side Democratic Club. There were also the times when she opened her heart and her apartment to a good friend. The young woman was studying piano under one of the top teachers in the country and she needed to practice for a number of hours each day. She played beautifully but only the brave can withstand hours of the same exercises. Betty was brave. It all worked out and eventually her playing inspired even Guye to study piano. Betty had to listen through the wall between the two apartments while he made the first steps toward playing the instrument. And listen she did.

Once she mentioned to him that maybe he needed to change tutors because he seemed to be stagnating. It was true. He was in a rut of sorts and he vigorously reapplied himself. Months later he bought an electronic keyboard with ear phones. It was meant to reduce the stress on her ears but she almost took offense to it. She mentioned that she loved to hear his progress and that he was beginning to play quite well. She missed hearing him. Of course, Betty already played piano and she was an excellent reader. Eventually, her ageing Steinway Baby grand would be given to a young man who lived in the same building.

In the early years and as years flew by Betty spent much of her time helping others. She blamed herself for the early failure to convince tenants in the building to buy their apartments. She felt it was a big mistake and maybe she was right. But she wasn't responsible. She twisted no one's arm. She only gave them the facts as she perceived them at the time and if she was wrong, well, aren't we all sometimes a little wrong? As her fortunes rose she no longer had to ask Guye for a loan of carfare to get to and from work. She was able to afford her own cable television connection. She no longer had to depend on his help from a wire passed through a hole in the wall between the two apartments? She was always afraid of not having enough money to live out her golden years.

She always said that she hoped to die before the funds ran out or inflation and medical bills consumed it and left her a pauper. Betty had helped a lot of other people too. From Pearl, the first part - time maid who'd worked for her and introduced her to Abyssinian Baptist Church in Harlem to a man she'd met while she was working as a volunteer at Riverside Baptist. It was difficult to see Pearl move south and even more difficult when she fell victim to a murderer's scheme of some sort.

But Betty rebounded and put it all in proper perspective. It was her way of dealing with things. She never stayed down for the count. And she wouldn't let Guye do it either. She even convinced him to attend Church with her at Riverside Baptist. They took the bus there and back on two occasions. She paid his small contribution to the plate with a check of her own. Yes, she helped folks and she had worked as a volunteer at the church even after her own retirement at a Wall Street Brokerage House. There her boss had come to depend on her. As his Secretary, she must have been the best. Those had been some of the best years of her life, she often said to Guye. And he knew that to be true as they were also a few of the years he'd known her when she wasn't suffering from one illness or another. Those had been the boyfriend years. Guye could remember at least three. And those had also been the years when she rode her bicycle to work on Wall Street and back home nearly every day of the week. The times of Dr. C. and relatively few asthma related problems. Dr. C. had been recommended by a good friend of Guye's. He was actually a physician who specialized in pediatric allergies but the friend had introduced him to Betty and they clicked. In later years she would often mention Dr. C.

Then there was the time she'd met a new beau. That was the term she used for all her close male friends. With his blessings, she decided to go ahead with a cosmetic procedure. Not facial. Just a little problem that had become her nemesis. It wasn't very successful and the swelling and after effects would last for years. Much longer than the beau.

She enjoyed it at the time. There were other beau's too. She liked relationships, she told Guye but when they were over. Well, they were over. He'd hear about the good times and the worst of them but she never complained. Only once did he ever remember Betty mention that she wished she'd married. Guye wasn't sure whether she was serious or just joking. She said she'd had the opportunity to marry a very wealthy man but she had turned him down. She even showed Guye her final letter to the man.

Even after she retired from Wall Street she remained active; co - purchasing a house in upstate New York and then getting her driver's license and buying an automobile. She'd drive up there at least once a month, especially around holidays and in nice weather. She grew and planted seedlings in a box on the window sill of her bedroom. There, she would nurture them until she could plant them on the grounds of the get- away that she shared with Margaret and two of their friends. She'd leave the plants to be watered by Guye while she was away. He knew nothing about watering plants and would often make a mess of things but Betty never said anything about it.

There was the automobile accident that nearly took her life and soon the country house was sold but in later years she'd take the bus from Manhattan to Great Barrington, Massachusetts after Margaret and Ted moved there. She'd leave on Friday and drive back with Margaret on Tuesday. She absolutely adored her nephew Ted and she planned tiny surprises for him. When still a toddler she had baby sat him. Watching over him like the good aunt she was. Guye had fond memories of Betty and the little blond child she was so proud of. Anyone could tell that she believed he was someone special.

Betty was the best at everything she did. Over the years she'd learned to be a good cook and she sometimes prepared dinner for Guye and for a couple of friends. The baked bread that she called Monkey -bread was delicious, as were most of her baked under-takings. Those dinner evenings were always pleasantly spent and if one of them could not make the date at dinner time Betty delivered the meal to the door still warm and fresh. Betty never forgot birthdays. There was always an invitation for dinner to her friends and most times she baked them a birthday special. In Guye's case it was a Lemon Meringue pie. All for himself.

The only obstacle was that she never wanted to accept anything for herself.

She would not even accept payment for her time as a Notary Public. She would spend an hour talking with whomever needed her services and she would offer them tea and cookies. He'd never paid her and he didn't know anyone else who had either. She always made certain she renewed the license before it expired. It was one more link to the community. An opportunity to be useful and to exchange ideas and Betty loved every minute.

Betty kept up a whirlwind pace that would have been a challenge for a person in the best of health. She arose early and sometimes went to bed quite late. She was always involved in one project or another. She bought a PC at a late age and then learned to navigate it. She was proud when she made The New York Times her Home

Text Me From Manhattan

Page and it was not unusual for her to read the entire paper on line. She took courses at the Public Library. She was never too tired to pop a tape into her VCR to get a copy of something she wanted Guye to enjoy or to be aware of in the world.

Mostly, it was stuff from Channel 13, PBS. A Bill Moyers piece or Frontline or something new in the medical field. He'd come in from work to find the customary note taped to his door. It would read for example: Dear Maurice, I have taped this program about genocide in Rwanda. Thought you might be interested. LUF, me. Over the years there would be dozens and dozens of similar notes or notes reminding him to ring her once he was in the house so that he could have a hot meal delivered to his door, or a note about a book she had for him to read at his leisure. She was an incredible next door neighbor. She was an unbelievable friend.

Besides the customary gift she exchanged by mail each year with her long- time Japanese friend Yoshiko, she would spend time making quilts and even making her own outfits to wear. She sent birthday and Christmas cards and sometimes money. Always a thank you to reciprocate for the time someone took to call or write of chat with her on the telephone. She was always grateful for the smallest things and Guye had long ago given up on trying to give her presents. Betty gave him the impression that somehow she felt that she was not worthy of even the smallest gift and so he kept his mouth closed and tried to sneak in an extra favor here and there. But he had to be careful about it. She was always alert and sensitive about such things and she'd fuss a little about it. Helping her sort through and put in order her medications was one way to do it.

Helping her with her various projects in small ways was another. She could never make up her mind about which colors and patterns to use for Margaret and Ted's quilt and she'd ask his opinion several times. She always let him read important letters she wrote to her employers and to friends and family. Not that she wasn't great at it. She was fantastic. It was her way of confirming to him that she valued his opinion. He had worked at the U. N. as personal Secretary to an Ambassador or two and she was as proud of that as he was.

She was allergic to flowers and anything else made her feel uncomfortable. "Betty you are hopeless," he'd tell her. And they'd laugh together.

The only thing Guye ever remembered her accepting from him were the few dollars he'd lent her from time to time in the early years or some adhesive tape. Sometimes an onion. Then, there was the time she told him that she got tired standing on the Saturdays she braved the world and the elements to protest the War in Iraq. She spent hours each week making and re-making the placards she carried to protest the war and handing out the buttons she ordered at her own expense and then sold without profit. It was no easy task and she always asked him his thoughts. Not much, just enough to keep him interested and around.

Walking on Broadway a few days after she mentioned she tired early in the afternoons, Guye spotted a folding seat for sale. It was not very big but just enough for her to take the load off her feet. When he presented it to her she was happy and was just about to offer payment for it when something happened to distract the two of them.

As he left her at her door she looked as though she remembered but he hurried to change the subject. She never said anything more about the chair. At last he'd managed to do something for her! She always wanted to give, give and give. She accepted nothing in return. Just friendship maybe love if you had it to spare. If anyone deserved to be loved it was her. She gave it. How could anyone not give it back?

As a hopeful musician Guye was devastated to learn that he'd lost almost all of the hearing in his left ear to autosclerosis. It was getting worse and soon it was predicted that he'd be half deaf. Betty told him about her friend who'd had an operation to partially restore her hearing. She too had the degenerative condition. Off he went to a specialist to try a surgical procedure to correct his hearing. It was scheduled. Early, the day of the operation Betty accompanied him to the hospital and waited until he was admitted. The results were more than modest and his hearing was almost restored in full. As usual, she would take no credit for her participation in the success.

She'd always been a sickly thing, she had informed him many times. There always seemed to be one illness after another trying to sap her strength. But Betty was made of sterner stuff than any physical ailment. If she had to be in the hospital for a couple of days she would simply ask Guye to keep an eye on the apartment. If she was locked out she would have the doorman ring him on the telephone or intercom. By the time she got to the 4th floor her door would be open and the light would be on in the foyer.

As Betty grew more and more weak from the ravages of one illness or another her friend grew more and more concerned about something she had confessed to him at one time. She told him she did not believe in God. He remembered being shocked by the news. It was the first time anyone had said that to him. In fact, he'd always imagined that anybody who attended Church as often as she once had must surely be a God -fearing woman. But he did not press her about it. He sat there and listened quietly. It was her business and who was he to judge? That in itself would have been against what he believed in about Jesus and about the Higher Power. She'd told him that even before she took him to Riverside Church to meet and greet new friends. After all, she had done it.

She said it was the political thing to do but on the Sundays they'd gone to Riverside she sat next to him singing the songs she knew well and reciting the lines when prompted by the Minister. She looked like she was enjoying every minute of it and Guye liked to think that she was. After the services were over she stood in line and shook hands with the Minister; introducing Guye to him. They seemed to be well acquainted with one another and it was then that Guye remembered that Betty had been a volunteer at the church. She had served beverages and goodies there along with her good friend Annette.

She liked the Minister she said to Guye but she didn't particularly care for his style or his politics. It would be after her death before he learned that the two of them had had a confrontation of sorts when she was doing volunteer work. Guye liked the Minister's style a lot but of course he didn't know him and he and Betty didn't quibble about that point. Friends, he'd learned from her, never argue. At least they didn't call it that.

Once there had been a misunderstanding about a question that concerned race. The discussion hadn't ended with them on the same page but they got over it. In the future they were careful to avoid any topic which might cause dissention between them. Life was too short. They both could agree on that much. And besides, there were never any subjects that he could remember evading. They were friends after all. They found common ground on every topic. In fact, they were so comfortable around one another that following her cosmetic surgery to remove varicose veins Betty had proudly shown him her lack of scars. All the way to the hip! And after she went for her mastectomy to remove the second cancerous breast, she had no trouble revealing to him the large X across her chest. It was better after all to have a living friend than a dead one. They'd laughed about the scar.

Time was passing and the friends were growing older. Time it seemed was overtaking everything in their lives. In his life there were a series of deaths. Some seemed early and untimely while others were expected but nonetheless difficult to cope with. Betty liked that word: cope. She tried to cope with everything in her life as well as in the lives of others close to her. She was always there for them. Guye had keys to her apartment and she had keys to his. He imagined it was the same with her friend Suzanne down the hall. She was a registered nurse and a widow. From what Guye knew Suzanne's husband had been a Holocaust survivor and a well-respected psychiatrist in his own right. Like his wife Suzanne he was a kind man. Guye remembered him best for the pet dog he walked every day. The dog carried a stick in its mouth and was trained to keep it there. Suzanne was a wonderful person and a member of Betty's inner circle of supporters and friends. More and more she depended on her circle for support.

There was her relationships with Margaret and Teddy but she didn't want to be a bother to Margaret. She'd privately say this to Guye but as active and visible as she'd once been, she now preferred to associate with only a few people. Betty balked at having a visiting nurse. For years, she'd simply set it aside saying it was too expensive. Or, that there was nothing much for anyone to do. They'd get under one another's skin. She still looked forward to having her apartment cleaned once a week but after Gladys became disabled and too occupied with her own familial problems, Betty said no one could ever clean her place as effectively.

On her eightieth birthday Margaret planned a nice celebration. It was held at the Chinese Restaurant Betty was most familiar with as she had ordered take out from the place over a number of years. Everything was set and all were looking forward to it. But Betty told Guye she didn't want to attend. Margaret was making too much fuss over an old birthday party. For a few days it was touch and go as she vacillated between accepting and denying others the chance to celebrate her. On one day she called him to her apartment where she was in tears. It wasn't fair of her sister - in - law to plan these things without her approval, she told him. She was ill and she didn't feel up to facing all the people and the pressure. But Guye was patient with her and in the end she agreed to go. She looked lovely and thoroughly enjoyed herself. There were members of her family in attendance and some of the best friends she had left in this world. She was ecstatic and talked about the event for a long time afterwards.

The world was becoming uncertain and as changes occurred Guye's fortunes fell. He found himself depending more and more on his friend Betty for moral and sometimes financial support. As usual, she was positive about the outcome of things but he was apprehensive.

There had been serious alterations in the way business was being conducted on his biggest contract. The old guard had left and that meant his long time business friend and colleague. She became sick with cancer and died just a little less than two years after her retirement. It was a blow from which he was still reeling.

As difficult as she had become in her later years, she had always appreciated Guye as a friend and a hard worker. But as things go in life she was no longer on this Earth and her replacement, a woman from Costa Rica, seemed not eager to see anyone of Guye's background in a position of authority. She seemed like a nice enough person as far as he could tell. He thought it because she felt more comfortable with people who spoke her own language. Whatever it was, she'd never really warmed to him and that was unusual. He'd never really known anyone who didn't like him after they got to know him as a person. It was a blow. She'd cut back on most of the responsibilities he had been given at the school and with the cuts she had naturally reduced payments.

Sometimes he had to ask Betty for a small loan just to meet his payroll. There was nowhere else to turn.

It was sometimes a struggle to repay her but the loans were always paid. She never pressed him for the money.

And then, just when it seemed as though things would right

themselves. The absolute worse happened. The worse economic times since Betty's early years in the Great Depression struck. Guye was not prepared for it. It was a death blow for his future as her next door neighbor. Yes, he would rebuild and begin a new life he told her. But it could not be there. He would no longer be able to live next door. Just eating and keeping the lights on would be a struggle and he could not pay the rent. As her friend sat there on his final night in his apartment it was clear that Betty had a lot on her mind but they were close enough to know when to pry and when to remain silent. She did mention that she felt it an ugly world they were living in. She had lived through the best and the worst of times she said, and it was not necessarily the state of the world economy she was referring to but the attitudes of the occupants on the planet. People seemed just a bit meaner. A wee bit harder and crueler. A tiny bit less concerned about the feelings and the plight of others.

Betty didn't want to talk about politics or even current events any longer. At one time these had been among her favorite subjects but it was all too much for her now. Too overwhelming, too depressing. The reading had ceased as well but this was mainly due to her lack of strength and concentration she told him. She just could not focus anymore and the last book they'd shared had been Fox Butterfield's "All God's Children". Betty didn't finish reading it. It was too depressing, she said.

Still, there were days when she felt fairly strong. Then, she would freshen herself and cook a little something or just make tea for the two of them. They would sit there often, in the little kitchen and talk. Talk until the telephone rang. It would be from Margaret. She lived for Margaret's call every evening between 8:30 and 9:00 and Margaret never disappointed. "She's a good girl," Betty would say. "She must be," he'd say to her, grinning his approval.

This would also be his cue to cut the evening short and he'd whisper goodnight, now giving the customary peck on the cheek.

It was refreshing to see how she had grown to those moments. Years earlier she would never have offered more than a handshake to a friend.

Now, as he stood there saying goodbye, Guye felt as if he was saying goodbye to Betty in more ways than one. He knew he'd see her and call her again and he talked about coming by her apartment just to take her outdoors to Central Park. She could sit in the wheelchair with a nice throw over her legs to keep warm and as they walked, they could both enjoy the sunshine. It was a great idea but it would never happen. Somehow he'd known that much in his heart. She was too proud to sit in a wheelchair and be rolled around. Even by a friend or a relative. And he'd noticed something else besides her inability to remember things from one moment to the next.

She might remember things that had happened as a child or something that had occurred last week but she might not remember what was said even 2 minutes earlier. She also talked a lot about dying. She hadn't done that in a couple of years. "Oh, why don't I just die and get it over with?" Back then she'd said that only during her most agonizing moments. But now it was different. Now, she'd added something extra, "I'll be glad when I'm dead."

Yes, he said to himself looking at her. This is different and I am powerless to do anything about it. Gone was the promise that he'd be there to watch over her if she ever became bedridden. No longer could he state that he would have a door cut into the walls between their two apartments so that he would be there to help nurse her if she ever needed him. He'd always known that she'd never allow it but it made them both feel a little better when he'd say it.

Guye could only watch as his lifelong friend's condition deteriorated. Each time he saw her he noticed the change. Until even the sparkle in her beautiful blue eyes began to fade. It was heartbreaking and for the first time in their relationship he had no reply to give. The old talk seemed somehow hollow and insufficient now. It seemed pointless to try to say he'd be there for her when she was 100 or more. She didn't want to live that long and he knew that he might not make the date either.

Just saying goodbye, he'd forced himself to look at her. From deep inside he willed the mask of bravery to hold up just a few minutes longer until he could close her door. Until, in private and out of her watchful eyesight he could allow his composure to crack into a thousand tiny pieces. The debris of memories and despair; the memorabilia of a thousand days of happiness.

After a sleepless night in the apartment Guye left the building before 8 A.M.

He'd planned it that way. He wanted to avoid saying goodbyes to the staff and other residents.

He would come back in a week or so and take care of the staff after all it was Christmas time and he had always managed to give them a gift of money. Sometimes, he'd given money and a bottle of cheer. But that had been in the old days. His finances no longer allowed him to do both. Walking quickly to the front of the lobby he left a bag with the doorman. It contained the cable boxes for the Cable Company whenever they called for them. They never did.

Then, for one final time he walked through the door and into the street. Guye was on his way to Penn Station where he would purchase a ticket to Albany, New York. His furniture would be delivered to the apartment his friends were holding for him.

The new place would be on the ground floor of the house and from there he would start his rebuilding process. But once he arrived in Albany the worse happened. The apartment was too small and uncomfortable. It was not at all what he'd imagined it would be.

Leaving his possessions in storage in a New Jersey warehouse he continued to look for a suitable apartment in Albany and in New York City. Sadly, one or two additional visits to the State Capital would decide for him the folly of moving there to live. Living in Albany required a car. It was something he should have known in advance. It was a question of poor planning and desperation but in the end, his heart wasn't in it.

Guye could blame no one for what had happened- not even himself. It was all new to him. He'd never had to do this and had never thought he would have to at this stage of his life. If anything, he had put too much pressure on himself in thinking he could just pick up and go. It was all a little much to cut off friends and familiar surroundings. Even for the desperate and the foolhardy. He realized he still had a lot to learn about living. Maybe things had been too easy for him all those years. Perhaps, he needed to be shaken a bit to get things moving. Like a container of juice or a bottle of ketchup. In any event, this was not the end of The world for him.

There were a few bright angles in the equation. One was that back in the City, he'd be nearer his friend Betty. She seemed to be in failing health but whenever they talked on the telephone she offered some kind of support. He tried not to bother her. He tried not to ask for help as he knew her condition was not improving but a few times he had no other alternative. She never tired of him. To her credit she never complained. He'd resolve not to discuss his situation with her but she insisted. She wanted to hear how he was doing and what it was like to be out of money and out of work in New York City.

"Go see if the Chinese Restaurants are hiring." "Maybe you can wash dishes there or something," she would suggest. It was vintage Betty Lou. Always trying to be helpful to others, especially to her friends.

Always suggesting something that might be helpful. She couldn't help it. She hated seeing anyone in need; if she could have she would have saved the world from its miseries.

In early March Guye learned that his friend had been admitted to the hospital. She had been there many times over the years. He'd gone with her in the ambulance at least twice before and once in a taxi. He had waited with her in the emergency rooms. When she required admission he'd stay there until she dismissed him with a wave of the hand. When necessary he'd picked her up in a cab when she was discharged.

He wasn't too alarmed about the latest admission. But the longer she remained in the hospital the more concerned he grew.

This time seemed different than the others. Not necessarily in the time it took for her to recuperate but in her lack of commitment to healing. It was the first and only time he regretted not being next door to her. Could his presence have made a difference? Betty always said he had given her encouragement and strength and maybe, just perhaps. ... He visited her several times as she recuperated in a nursing facility near her home.

At first it seemed to be a case of touch and go but with visits from Margaret and Suzanne she seemed to respond to her therapy. It took a few weeks longer than expected but soon, Betty was home again. It was where she wanted most to be and Guye stopped at her place to see her. He didn't stay long because she tired quickly. Just fifteen or twenty minutes the first visit. On the second visit she seemed withdrawn and disinterested in everything around her but she kept asking him how he was doing. She was concerned about that.

Guye moved in with his brother. The brother lived in Harlem and from there he tried calling Betty at least once a week. Spring came and went, then summer. No longer living next door, the friends had fewer opportunities to be in touch but that was the way it was sometimes with friends. Actually, it hadn't been so different when they lived next door to one another. They'd miss each other for a period of time and then suddenly, they would call or visit nearly every day for a while. One thing was certain, he thought of her every day and he was sure she thought of him.

Early on Election Day he realized that he had neglected to find a new polling place. Still living in Harlem at his brother's place he was using a Post Office Box for his mail. He decided to vote at the same place he'd voted for years. It was in his old neighborhood.

It seemed that on the morning of Election Day everything that could, would go wrong. He had scheduled to meet a friend for a few minutes and then go to 57th Street for art supplies. Afterwards, he'd go over to 102nd Street by bus and vote for his candidates. If he felt up to it, he'd stop in to see Betty for just a minute as she had weighed heavily on his mind the past couple of weeks. But at the last minute he had to change his plans just slightly. He reversed the entire plan. He went first to 57th Street before meeting his friend. Together, they continued on to vote.

It was fortuitous that it worked out that way because after a few minutes in the polling station he met an old friend from his former apartment building.

The first thing he told Guye was that Betty had passed! The news hit him like a thunderbolt! Guye was almost paralyzed with grief. Here he stood, inside a polling station ready to pull the levers and he is confronted with the news that his dear friend is dead. Maybe his last dearest friend left on the planet. Methodically, he completed his civic duty. But as he stood behind the curtain he heard the voice of Suzanne, another friend.

He heard the surprise in her voice when told the news that he was in the booth. She asked.

"Here, Guye is here?" He walked out of the booth and as they embraced Suzanne said,

"We've been trying to reach you for about ten days. We've

called and called but the number you gave us does not work." By us, she was speaking of Betty's sister - in -law. "We need an address and a phone number to reach you. Betty died ten days ago!" They stood there looking at each other. Trying to put on brave faces and searching to find something positive to say about what they both knew was something very negative in their lives.

Not because of her. Betty had died at home in her bed in what seemed to be under peaceful circumstances and that was great. She had often expressed the desire to be relieved of her pain and suffering and it appeared that her wish had been granted. They talked of old times and the dear friend that both had known and would now miss. She told him that she'd miss the dinners and the extra goodies and the talk and comfort of Betty being just next door. But he had already been missing these things for the better part of nine months. He hadn't got over it all but that day would come.

For a minute he was thinking of something else. He wasn't a deeply devout person but when it came to matters of the soul but he was a strong believer in the presence and the power of God.

Guye had been raised that way from an infant and it was something he could never change. He knew in his heart of his own commitment and he had been raised to keep it private but ever present. At the moment he was told of Betty's death he had thought of the time she told him she did not believe in God. What now, he asked himself? What now?

It wasn't until he was seated on the train that he remembered that the last few times they'd talked she had always mentioned God. In some small way she had mentioned Him and Guye recalled that during those times he had been surprised. He'd wanted to ask her about it but somehow he never got around to it.

Still, in his heart he knew that no one mentions God if they don't believe in His existence. And she must have felt His power.

How else could her own goodness and generosity be explained? It was a comforting thought and it made him feel good inside. There was something else that Suzanne had mentioned. Just before saying goodbye Suzanne told him that an attorney had been asking for his address and telephone number. And as he wrote his brother's number in her address book he wondered why.

He'd left Suzanne with a heavy heart and it seemed only minutes until he descended the train at 145th Street Avenue, and made his way toward his brother's place. There was a chill in the air and he felt suddenly alone. He needed to get in touch with Suzanne soon to pick up the coat he had left in Betty's place. They'd promised to keep in touch.

Soon after Guye received a letter in his Post Office Box. It was from the attorney Betty had always spoken about with so much praise. He had been Betty's friend for many years. She was like that. Once she liked someone she liked them and that was that. It took a great deal to change those feelings of trust. Guye opened the letter right there in the post office. He wondered again why Betty's friend would want to write to him. Maybe it was some last service he could perform for her. Maybe she didn't want to trust it with anyone but him. He wouldn't be surprised if that were the care. She had her priorities.

But it was a notice of Probate and it concerned her will. Betty had included him in her last will and testament. With his thumb and fingers anchored to his chin he stood there lost in thought.

She had mentioned something about this to him. But that had been more than a dozen years ago when they were both younger and she was healthier. Maybe he was healthier then too.

Whatever. He was certainly grateful to her for her kindness. Just for thinking that far ahead.

And he thought of something else. Of course he had no idea where the souls of people go when they leave this world. Or, who really knows who is right and who is wrong on that score. But there is one thing that Guye was now quite certain of. Wherever the good abide, surely they could not deny her knock at the door. His friend Betty was a true believer!

"But wilt thou know, O vain man, that faith without works is dead?"

New York City, NEW YORK - 18th November, 2009

NOW HEAR THIS

IT HAD BEEN days since she remembered being spoken to and she knew it had nothing to do with her crutch. That was the word her father always used to describe her protestations that she had not complied with his wishes because she hadn't heard him clearly. She had been born with a hearing deficiency, she told everyone, and they would just have to bear with her. In her youth she'd been taken to every hearing specialist in the area, and a few as far away as Pittsburg and Bethesda.

Not one of them had been able to find anything wrong with her. She had been tested for everything. From deafness due to hereditary reasons to nerve damage but the results were always the same.

It had finally been concluded that she was not in the least bit deaf. As her father had suspected, she was simply pretending to be deaf. It had cost him a great deal of time, money and effort to confirm and he was bitter. Her father would remain that way for the rest of his life. But that had been long ago. That was then and this was the now. An awful lot had changed since she was a girl fifty years ago. She had married and divorced and married twice more. From the first marriage she'd had kids of her own. Now her kids had children and they'd had kids too. She was now a grandmother at least four times over.

Although having two boys and three girls one could never be sure how many grands there were or might have been. Especially with the boys. Sometimes they didn't even know. She was just being real, she reminded folks. These were modern times and they called for a modern day approach to sexual issues. If others wanted to keep their heads in the sand…well, that was on them. There were so many things wrong in the world as far as she was concerned and they were not likely to improve in her lifetime.

"Why just look at what I've got to deal with every day," she'd complain to anyone and everyone.

"Nobody ever listens to what I have to say. I might as well be talking to myself." She always blamed technology for that lack of attention. In her day people only had radios to talk above. Now there were boom boxes and I-Pods, CD's and DVD's and Heavens knows what there'll be next week or next year. "That's all they ever do," she'd say to anyone who'd listen. "They play their music, smoke that stuff and beg.

Let's not forget the begging. They won't work in a pie factory eating pies but they always have their hands out begging. Everyone's always asking me for a favor and expecting me to do things for them when they know full well that I'm weak and sickly. It's no wonder I'm a poor woman. I've given away a fortune in my life time. It's not been easy living on a fixed income. There are so many expenses that need to be taken care of. But. I wonder if they ever give that any consideration," she said to Wesley.

Wesley was her husband and they had been married for fourteen years.

He was not the father of any of her children. He had been married twice before, and he had his own kids. They were all grown but they continued to call on him for favors. But Wesley was different from Linda. He never complained about his kids or about too much of anything. Not openly. Besides, Wesley knew very well what her other expenses were and none of them had anything to do with need. There was the full pack of cigarettes that, even against her doctor's orders she sort of smoked each day. Sometimes she left one or two of them burning in the ash trays around the house.

They would lay there smoldering: long oval -shaped ashes that poisoned the air and fell apart only when the ash tray was moved. There were the Pepsi Colas and Coca Colas she insisted upon drinking throughout the day and half the night, the sweets and the cakes and pies she indulged in every day and the compulsive purchasing of handbags and shoes, coats and hats and anything else that was not nailed to the shelves in the stores and shopping malls.

Wesley Armstead had come to expect little from his wife. That was the way it had been since they'd married and he supposed he was destined to live out his days with her.

Theirs had been a chance meeting and a short courtship. Both of them were in somewhat of a rut at the time and looking for something or someone new to give their lives a new meaning and direction. They had found comfort in one another's arms. There had been some opposition from her children. Particularly from one of the girls who was then having marital difficulties of her own and contemplating moving back to live with her mother. Melissa had taken it hard when her mother announced that she and Wesley had tied the knot three days earlier. He remembered it all too well.

After a brief City Hall ceremony the newlyweds had boarded a bus and taken a sightseeing trip around Manhattan Island. Afterwards there was a candlelight dinner at Tavern on the Green in Central Park and a horse drawn ride through the Park. Then, home to a late night toast to a bright tomorrow and romance. It all had been simple and not very costly. Just the way Wes Armstead liked things. Simple and uncomplicated. Not too much salt pork in the cabbage and not too many Chefs in the kitchen was the way he liked to put it. They were both too old for that honey-moon junk. They'd had their share of fun and partying and the next big celebration was probably going to be done by his heirs once they discovered he'd died and left them his insurance policy. Twelve years later he was beginning to re-think that decision. Perhaps he shouldn't leave the kids so much. They'd only fight over it. Then again, perhaps he'd made a mistake when he married for the third time. Sure, he loved Linda. That much she knew. Or, at least he hoped she did.

But something had changed with her. Linda was not the same person any longer. She was picky and irritable. She was also persistently demanding and rude to him and anyone who called her or stopped by the house. It had become embarrassing and he had taken to meeting his friends and acquaintances outside his house. It was sometimes inconvenient and uncomfortable but more and more he asked them not to call his home and to never, ever show up unannounced. After a while she would ask him why this one or that one never called anymore. Then she would blame him for being rude to his friends and to her. "Have you been borrowing money from anyone? People don't stop being friends for nothing. You HAD to do something to them," she would say.

"What do you want from me?"

He had shouted this at her many times. She could never answer this question. She honestly didn't know. All she knew was that whatever it was he could not provide it. He was not enough anymore. In fact, nothing was enough anymore and maybe nothing ever had been. She swore over and over that they could do a lot better if only Wesley would take the time to listen to her. To pay attention to her wants and needs like any decent companion would do. That was the way Linda put it. "Don't try to make me responsible for the way things are Wesley Armstead. You're the man of the family. At least you're supposed to be," she would say mockingly.

She was depressed when they were short of money. She was unhappy when they had enough money to do the extra things they both liked to do. And she always needed a little extra. She was unhappy when the kids called and of course unhappy when they didn't call. She had begun hanging up on everyone who called or demanding that someone else answer the telephone. "Why should I talk to them when they never listen to anything I have to say," Linda would complain. Whenever the telephone rang she'd call, "will someone pick up the phone?" She was referring to Wesley of course and lately his brother Gervais Armstead. No one else lived there.

Wesley's brother had found himself down on his luck and unable to remain in the apartment he had rented for the last thirty years but never owned. Reluctantly, he'd asked if he could take the spare room in his brother and sister - in –law's place until he could get on his feet again. They had enthusiastically agreed. At first. However, the longer it took for Gervais to re-cover the less welcome he was in their home. At least that was the impression his sister - in - law gave. It seemed to Gervais that the only time she was somewhat pleased was when he was required to pay much more than his share of the rent. Every Wednesday morning she awoke happy but after he'd paid the rent she miraculously reverted to her same impatient and demanding personality. She was insufferably impolite and abrasive to everyone. To her the world was fraught with greedy and demanding people who took and took from her and never gave back. That that was only her opinion but it was backed up by her scant knowledge of the Bible. She could quote excerpts from it at her convenience. After all she attended Bible study every Thursday night without fail. Sometimes the little group session would be held at her apartment and then the world would have to come to an abrupt halt. At least until the studies were over for the night. Sometimes Wesley didn't mind the study group. After all, he reasoned everyone had to have an outlet and a passion. It's what keeps us young and on our toes he told her.

But there were times when his wife would not want the studies held in her apartment. This was what really got to him. "Why don't you simply tell them a few days in advance?

Why do you insist upon keeping everything a secret until they are knocking on the door? Have a little consideration for the feelings of others, for Pete's sake!"

And there were other annoying things about Linda's behavior that stuck In Wes' craw. Like her penchant for meeting strangers on the streets and giving them her telephone number or address. Oftentimes, someone would call or ring the bell and ask for him by first and last name. It was so dangerous and totally thoughtless to do this.

Whenever he called her on it she would use the same excuse saying, "the Bible says that we should never turn strangers away from our door." "Yes, that's true," he'd reply. But the Bible was written several thousand years ago and this is 2009-Twenty-First Century-New York City. "You're living in Harlem my lovely, not in Canaan, 0009." Yes, Linda was a real work of art and she was becoming more and more refined at her gift. She seemed to relish the fact that she upset those closest to her with her constant criticisms and her mood swings. Her husband couldn't deny that over the course of their marriage her children had become somewhat of a burden. He wasn't blind he told her. "But why do you continue to do things for them if you are going to spend the next six months talking about it? I don't want to hear that any longer. Don't give them anything else and that will put a stop to all this nonsense.

If you don't want to answer the telephone then turn it off or unplug it. What do I care? No one calls me!"

Having succeeded in provoking him to anger, she would begin to cry and beg forgiveness. "I haven't felt well all day," she'd proclaim. "I don't know what's wrong with me tonight. I just feel so useless in this world. Maybe it would be better for everyone if I just got it over with and killed myself. Oh, why didn't I die when I had the hip replacement operation," she would moan. "I told you I didn't want to have anyone cutting on my body but you wouldn't listen and now I'm the one suffering."

It was clear to everyone close to her that Linda Collins-Armstead was out of control. She needed professional help. Professional help such as the kind she's been given when she'd had a mental breakdown before her marriage to Wesley Armstead. Then, she had been confined to a facility for the mental challenged for a period of two months. In several ways it seemed as though she'd made a remarkable recovery. But in others it appeared the reverse was true and in the waning months of the current year she was demanding that there be no visits from her children, no phone calls made or answered in the house and that all doors be kept bolted from sunrise to sunrise.

Linda didn't want to talk to anyone because she knew in advance what they wanted from her. She was afraid that she'd be asked to do someone a favor. She didn't want to watch TV because someone might knock on the door and know that she was at home. There could be no laughter inside and voices needed to be kept at a decent level. And that meant as low as possible. Just above a whisper.

And even though she loved them, all games shows, talk shows, the news, dramas and the like were off limits. Only soft music could be played in the apartment and that had to be jazz music from the 50's and 60's. Even then, the music had to be shut off when Linda Armstead went to bed. Everyone knew she had was unable to sleep when there were lights on or music playing. Her father had said as much when she was a little girl. Why wasn't anyone listening to her now?

It was Wesley's brother who first mentioned to him that what was going on with his wife was not normal.

Whether his brother was in the house or outdoors she seemed to find something to whisper about. "He's drinking too much again," she would say to Gervais. "He's not quite himself today because he's worried about his illness. Or, I hope he isn't at the bar around the corner or on the bench drinking with those bum friends of his."

She'd say these things to him in a voice that was no louder than a whisper. At first Gervais thought it was funny and he would whisper back to her. "I'm sure he's not drinking. He'll be upstairs in a few minutes sweetheart." And then he'd laugh to himself and try to hide his face. Eventually, he tried to leave the apartment before Wesley but it was no use. Linda began whispering to him even when Wes was at home.

As Thanksgiving Day drew neared the whispering grew worse on Linda's part and Gervais asked his brother to consider taking Linda to a specialist. Just to make sure that there wasn't a hidden problem.

"You never know about these things." he said to Wesley. But Wesley was preoccupied with the coming festivities and he replied that he'd mention it to her after the holidays. It was one of the only times of the year that Wesley considered his time: Thanksgiving, Christmas and the New Year. And his birthday of course. The other holidays he didn't give a damn about. He just didn't want anything to disrupt his days.

"Well, my brother," Gervais said. "Try to take her to a doctor as soon as possible because something strange is going on and I don't want you to be sorry later."

Just then the telephone rang and Linda whispered. "Tell them I'm not here." "Okay, you're not here."

Wesley whispered back. It was clear to Gervais that Wesley thought it was all a big joke.

"Is there anything wrong with the sound? I've been trying to hear what they're saying on the news but all I get is the picture." She was watching the six o'clock evening news and the question was addressed to her husband. "I've got the volume turned all the way up, look," he said. He showed her the graphic which confirmed the set was at full volume. "That's odd," she whispered. "Well, it should be no problem for you. You are the one who always says things are too loud around here. You've been watching TV on mute for years. You don't really want to hear what anyone has to say. Do you?"

When Linda didn't answer he said. "See, I told you so." And then Wesley laughed.

As Gervais had suggested things got progressively worse with Linda? Her crying fits were followed with thoughts of suicide and then periods of relative calm. By the middle of the first month of the year Linda had confined herself to her room. She would not even come out to go to the bath room unless Wesley made her take a bath. She was afraid that running the water or flushing the toilet would alert someone on the outside that she was at home and waiting to lend them some money or to do them a favor. On Valentine's Day Linda announced that she no longer had any need to turn on the radio or television. "After all," she whispered, "the light from the TV can be seen from any window across the street and the music could be heard from one apartment to the next. One never knows what the people next door might need. They might be fresh out of sugar or something."

On the last day of February Gervais moved. He'd seen enough and he was beginning to understand what was going on there. At first he didn't want to believe. But the longer he remained the clearer it became to him that Wesley knew his wife was suffering from mental challenges. There was no way he could have missed it. His brother knew and he had no intentions of taking her to get treatment. He was going to wait until she was too far gone and then he would call an ambulance and have her carted away like an old couch

She would be confined for the rest of her natural life.

Wesley would then live out the rest of his days in the apartment with his new love. A woman many years his junior. Gervais knew this to be true. How many times had he answered the telephone only to have it slammed down on the other end? It was a clear sign that someone wanted to speak to Wesley and to no one else in the apartment except Wesley. His brother couldn't fool him, he'd used the same old tactics dozens of times when he was seeing someone he had no business seeing or calling. Everyone does it he said to himself. He smiled remembering the old cliché: if a man answers, hang up! Well, that's his cross to bear and her misfortune Gervais thought.

I didn't make this keg of wine and I don't have to stick around to drink from it. He said his goodbyes to a tearful Linda and a happy Wesley and he left. It was February 29th, a one in four Year occurrence.

The moment his brother left Wesley put the balance of his plan into action.

He was once again in love. And the object of his affection was indeed younger than himself.

She was thirty -two years younger. In fact, that was her exact age. She was thirty –two and a stunner! Wesley had met her just the way he had met Linda. It was a chance meeting and now she wanted to be with him and he wanted to be with her. It was that simple. At first he had been reluctant to be unfaithful to his wife of fourteen years but Linda's persistent nagging was enough to drive anybody away from her.

Linda was making him old! And he hated living under the same ceiling. It was a pity he had to admit that but even her own children had stopped calling and trying to visit them. If it was left to Linda they would grow senile and old and maybe die within hours of one another right there in their home. Oh, she would be ecstatic about that, Linda would. It would complete her movie. She was ever the drama queen, Wesley told everyone. And she was as mad as a hatter. He, Wesley knew this but there was little he could do to help her. She didn't want his help. She didn't want anyone's help.

He'd asked around and he'd been told that there was plenty of help available to people in her condition but first they had to be sure she was completely and certifiably insane. She needed to do something to push her over the edge. She was almost there but maybe he needed to give her a little help. Just a little. He thought this as he turned up the volume on the radio and switched on the television. He thought of it again as he left the lights burning night and day. Wesley made sure that everything he said around the house was in a whisper and eventually he stopped speaking to her at all. He'd just get in her face to make sure she was watching him and then he would move his lips pretending he was actually speaking. He enjoyed watching the look of puzzlement on her face as she struggled to understand his words and intentions.

Abruptly he stopped speaking to her at all.

Wesley wrote everything he said on a piece of paper and handed it to her. Then, he'd leave the house laughing and content in the knowledge that he was close to achieving his goal. The wait would not be long.

On St. Patrick's Day there were several phone calls and since Linda no longer answered the telephone she didn't bother to pick up. Wesley was not at home and she imagined he was at a bar drinking with his friends. He'll be along soon and I'll whisper to him that someone's been calling.

It's probably one of the kids asking for something that I haven't got, she said to herself. But the phone kept ringing and when Wesley was not at home by six o'clock, Linda turned on the answering device. Whoever called could leave a message. Her husband would return the call once he got home. Maybe it was important and someone he needed to speak with.

It wasn't long before the telephone was ringing again and she let the machine answer. Linda sat there shocked.

"Hello, Wes honey." It was a female voice. "I just wanted you to know that I miss you so much.

I'll be back in town next Tuesday. We can meet as usual at my place and spend a few hours together if you'd like. Oh, and Wes honey, I do need you to pay the rent and the car note like you did last month sweetie. Please." Linda could not believe the message she'd just heard. She got up and went over to the machine where she replayed the message again and again. There was no mistake. The message was for her husband Wesley. Wesley Armstead, her husband of fourteen years was having an affair. Committing adultery and being used by a much younger woman. And he was spending her money because Wesley had no real cash. He had only his monthly social security check which he needed to use for bills in the house. How could he pay someone's rent and car note? Wesley didn't own a car.

For two hours Linda sat on the couch thinking about what she had heard and when Wesley finally came in the door she got up and went to bed. Just before she closed the door she said to him, "goodnight, husband." Wesley didn't hear her however. As usual, Linda was whispering again. It took him a few minutes to realize there was a message on the machine. He sat in the chair next to the sofa and called China. She was visiting relatives in Chicago and they'd agreed not to be in touch with one another until the day she arrived back in New York City. Why was the girl calling him at home?

She was young, carefree and in love. All of this was completely understandable to Wesley but she also knew he was a married man and although Linda was sickly and hard of hearing she wasn't stupid.

He reminded her of these things. "Please baby, don't call like that again," he begged her. Wes hung up the phone and erased the message. That was a close call, he said to himself. China could have ruined everything with her lack of tact and discretion. They were lucky Linda had not intercepted the call or listened to the taped message. His goose would have been cooked. Linda wasn't the type to sit back and let herself be used. She wouldn't just watch her marriage go down the drain. Linda would do something and he was afraid to think of just what that something might be.

But Linda had heard everything and from the moment she knew, she began to accelerate her own plans to get rid of the problems in her life. Over the next few months Linda put her scheme in action. When her husband turned the radio or television volume up- she turned it down.

If she unplugged the phone and he plugged in again Linda unplugged it once more. She was careful to make sure she did this without Wesley's awareness. She enjoyed watching him scratch his head with wonder at the sudden silence in the apartment. It was a game of cat and mouse and she was determined not to be the one who got caught. The second phase of her plan was to make him believe she was now stone deaf. No matter what he said to her she always threw her hands up in exasperation and then handing him a pencil and paper she would indicate that he needed to write it down. Linda hid things from her husband.

She hid things that he knew he'd just placed in a particular place in the house: shaving equipment and a tooth brush. She'd hide one sock or one of his shoes. Linda would do anything to make Wesley start wondering if he was losing his mind. She'd hide stuff and when he left the room for a few seconds it would mysteriously reappear. It was unnerving. But it was a brilliant ploy on Linda's part. Soon poor Wes didn't know if he was coming or going. He began to stutter and look around him. He checked everything twice and then tiptoed back into the room to make sure Linda was not playing tricks on him. She never allowed him to catch her. Wesley didn't realize that his wife Linda had been playing this game all he life. She had perfected a perfect scheme. A scheme begun when she was a little girl. A scheme that had worked for her through two previous marriages. She'd won then and she would win this time too.

Eventually, Wesley began to lose interest in going out to the bar or to visit with friends. The two would sit in the apartment in complete silence. The only time there would be other than the basic movements was when he went downstairs to the mailbox or left the house to purchase food. Most of the time he would sit in the house a nervous wreck of a man. He'd stare out the window or at the walls. Wes was always staring. As if he'd lost something and was waiting for it to appear again through the walls or the floor. There was almost no communication now. Not even with pen and pencil. Sometimes he'd try to talk to Linda but it was to no avail. Linda couldn't hear him and he couldn't make her understand him in any other way.

Soon Wesley couldn't make anyone else understand either. Whenever he went out of the house people looked at him and whispered. It was the last thing he needed to see them doing. Of course no one suspected or knew why they should not whisper. How could they have known?

Months and seasons turned into another but nothing changed inside the apartment of Linda and Wesley Armstead.

Eventually, the children stopped trying to call or visit. The mail remained in the box until it was overflowing or until it was returned to the Post Office. Most time it was given to the Super who placed it on the doormat of apartment 1- D. When this happened someone opened the door. A hand reached out to gather it quickly before the door slammed again.

No one was ever seen. Even the occasional visits to the local supermarket and pharmacy ceased. Foods supplies were ordered in bulk every three or four months and placed outside the door. But then, even the deliveries came to a halt. Occasionally, residents on the floor would hear the sound of knocking and knocking on the door. Apparently, one of Linda or Wesley's children had come to see what had become of them. They'd arrive to learn why they would not answer the telephone or the doorbell. It was clear that they were in the apartment because from the street one could see the lights being turned on or off. But soon even light bills went unpaid and service was suspended. The only thing that continued to be paid regularly was the rent. Each month on the first, the rent arrived by check to the landlord's address. Sometimes it was paid before the end of the month. They were there the landlord informed callers. And as long as they paid the rent and the increases he would let them alone. They had done nothing wrong. They had committed no crime.

Nobody knows how long this might have gone on had it not been for the fire. On the night of July 4th someone threw a firecracker through a window on the first floor of the building. A child's prank or a fool's, it did little damage. For safety reasons the fire department asked everyone in the building to leave their apartments. Just to be certain there were no smoldering wires etc. They knocked on doors and forced all the residents into the street for an hour while they and the police department searched each unit.

Someone noticed that the occupants of apartment 1-D were not answering the door. There was talk that they'd been acting strangely and that someone inside might have been responsible for the fire. The landlord was called to deliver keys or pay the cost of having his door knocked down. He delivered the keys. No one was prepared for what they discovered inside the apartment of Wesley and Linda Armstead!

When Patrolman Raymond Griggs knocked on the door of 1-D he had an odd feeling, He'd always been able to predict when something unpleasant was going to happen to him or to others around him. It was a special gift his mother said he'd inherited from his grandfather. True or not it had served him well for all of the twelve years he had served in the City's police department. He recalled that it had kept him from being in the line of gunfire at least three times. The count might even have been higher. Griggs was just trying to be a good cop and complete one more day so that he could hurry home to enjoy the evening of the Fourth with the wife and twin teenaged girls.

He thought no one had heard him as he stood knocking on the door of 1-D. He knocked harder and harder. No one opened the door but he felt he was being watched through the viewer. "Police Department. Open The Door." He repeated the order. "Police Department, Open Up or we'll break it down." He then gave one last warning and announced that he had keys and was coming in. It was only then that the door opened. A small thin figure stepped away to allow him to enter.

Nothing in all of his days on the force could compare with the stench and the disorder he and his colleagues witnessed. In fact nothing he'd ever seen or learned in the police academy had prepared him for this. There were boxes and cans everywhere. Paper and garbage lined the floors almost knee deep.

Clothing, furniture, pots and pans were strewn around the apartment as if no one had lived there for a decade or more. The odor was suffocating and the air was unhealthy to breathe Even walking was dangerous. But they had jobs to do and they turned to the figure of standing silently beside them and asked if there was anyone else in the apartment. They'd been told that there were two people living there. "Where is he or she or it," they demanded?

It was the first time Patrolman Griggs had a chance to actually look at the person he was addressing And he quickly drew in his breath.

He looked at Mrs. Linda Armstead. And she was a total wreck. With unkempt hair and broken teeth, layers of torn and unwashed clothing: her body emaciated. All Linda needed was a broom to complete the description that immediately came to his mind. Although she seemed to be mouthing words, she seemed unable to speak. At least unable to be heard. He and his partner followed her gaze as she directed them to the room that had once served as the scene of so many happy memories for Linda and Wesley Armstead. He was in there, she indicated.

Patrolman Griggs strode the five or six steps to the room and pushed it open. Then he stepped back and pulled it shut again. "Call an ambulance or somebody. Call a doctor or whoever it is who takes care of these damned things," he said in a choked voice. "Holy Toledo! I don't need to see this!" He turned toward Linda. "How long has he been like that, ma'am? How long has your husband been almost dead?"

Patrolman Raymond Griggs didn't want or need to see it but he had seen it. He had seen the skeletal shape of a man sitting up in the bed. He was alive and his eyes appeared twice their size in a face that was emaciated. But the eyes were staring as though he could no longer see his hand in front of him. If you could call hands the objects dangling from his coat - hanger like shoulders arms or hands. He had never seen pictures of anyone who looked that way unless they were photos of the dead. But the man was alive. He was barely alive but he was breathing.

Linda Armstead stood there taking in the scene. She wasn't worried. Wes would be fine. Her husband would be just fine and she would too. After all she had done nothing wrong. All she had done was save her marriage and her husband from all those unnecessary intrusions in their lives. Sometimes it is up to the woman to do these things. Wesley had been a naughty boy and he'd tried to run off with that tramp. But Linda had put a stop to it. She had taught him a lesson. She didn't speak to him for a year and when that seemed not to be working she was forced to tie Wesley to the bed for his own good. What did he know about taking care of himself?

And that bitch! Well, she only wanted to use him. She only wanted Wes to spend his money on her. But Wesley didn't have any money. Didn't the tramp realize that?

It was she, Linda who had the money and it was she who had saved her marriage and their beautiful home. Linda had put a stop to the designs of that woman. And Linda didn't understand what these people were doing in their apartment! What did they want of her?

What did they want with her Wes?

Why hadn't they left them alone? Why had the doctors not let her die when she had her hip replaced all those years ago? Well, she'd show these officers she was not to be trifled with. Linda Collins Armstead would show them. She would not speak. She wouldn't say a word because she couldn't hear them. Didn't they know she had a hearing problem? They would just have to bear with her because her father had been wrong. She had been born that way!

THE END

New York City, New York
November 10th, 2009 - 3:12 P. M.

SWEET - POTATO PIES

HALLELUJAH! IT WAS check day again and the magic was back. I knew that because at 8: ll there was a rap at my door. Still half asleep, I managed a sleepy good morning to my sister -in-law as she pronounced that the day had arrived. She'd hardly taken the time to mumble a proper greeting before she reminded me that it was time to get dressed and make a hasty dash to the bank and back. She wanted to get an early start. It was imperative that she shop for more clothes or jewelry before buying the supply of cigarettes using the monthly rent I paid her and my brother for the little space I temporarily occupied in their apartment. "After all business is business," she laughed. She tried to make a joke of it but she needn't have bothered. I knew what time it was in more ways than one.

Like so many others on the Hill and across the country, she appeared to have forgotten her vows of frugality made last check day and reinforced only the day before. They had been replaced by the flyers from newspapers announcing the latest sales. Gone were the struggles and the sacrifices of the previous ten days. Gone were the plans to be more thrifty and deliberate with the small monthly income that fell well below the government's poverty classification.

Gone too was the budget planning that living on a fixed income forced from the retired and just plain tired souls doing everything possible to make ends meet in an ever increasing world of inflation and temptation. "As long as the important bills are taken care of "had become the by-word once more. It was a repeated phrase borrowed from the month before and from the months before that. For the moment an infectious sore on too many lips. Tossed about by too many minds anxious to play out the joy of the day and perhaps a few days after, without the constant worry of not having enough.

Only the most prudent would make it to the next check day with enough. It wasn't an easy thing to do but a few would manage to limp to the finish line. Others, more foolish and carefree would spend, spend and spend again during the next 24 hour. Always saving a little for a least one hell of a weekend blast before the reality of it all took hold. The most foolhardy would dip into the bill money. The light bill would go unpaid or half used and even the rent. It was always harder to get to the weekend with a little cash whenever the checks arrived on Mondays and Tuesdays. For some, no matter how careful, the money always seemed to come and go like a flash storm on a summer's day or the piles of plowed snow on the city's streets in March. Snow that always melted in the warm sunlight along with the hastily made snow men in the parks. But today none of this seemed to be on anyone's mind. It was Monday, March 1st. It was check day and all was right with the world.

I stood there in front of the check cashing place awaiting the arrival of my own meager funds which were being brought to me compliments of my friend. We were sharing a mailbox together and it was his turn to check it for import mail and act like the

Pony Express. One could hardly call this small sum of money important but it was necessary. Necessary since with no other present income or prospects for any other in the near future my ship would sink. But it would be gone in a few hours. The only difference being that none would be spent on good times. I could hardly afford even this small luxury.

My friend was late and for sixty-five minutes I stood outside the establishment and observed the comings and goings about me. I had arrived at the appointed time. The 11 o'clock hour had not been my choice but then again it was not my call. I had only a few blocks to walk and my friend was coming by bus from further away. I waited good-naturedly and with patience. At least I did for the first half hour before, remembering his past habits I became more and more annoyed. He was no respecter of time. I struggled to dismiss the thought from my mind, doing everything humanly possible to remain positive but it was difficult. To make matters worse, I realized that with the temperature already in the mid-forties, I had probably dressed too warmly. Trying not to focus on my discomfort, I amused myself watching those like myself who had made an early start. I had been delighted to assist an elderly lady who somehow could not step over the small mound of snow piled in front of the mail box. Even with her cane she seemed unable to get close enough. She wasn't sure if it was an active box. I walked over to it and read out loud for her that they picked up every day Mondays through Fridays - 1 P.M. and on Saturdays at 1:15. Even with my reassurances she remained cautious as I prompted her to close the lid and open it again to be sure her envelope had fallen down the chute.

It was her rent check or some important utility bill she was mailing she announced to no one in particular and she couldn't afford to have it lost or late in arriving. I knew from experience that landlords and bill collectors could be unforgiving, even in hard times. Courage up, she dropped the mail in the box, then stood there looking at it as though she was saying farewell to a loved one who was leaving on a long voyage. Finally, she thanked me and walked away. Turning once more to observe another middle- aged woman anxious to do her mailing, approaching to drop her own letters into the blue chute which swallowed her mail like some voracious 4-legged chubby monster anxious to begin an early lunch of envelopes and stamps.

Leaning against the plate glass window which boasted a backdrop of 'come on posters' it enticed check cashers to try one plan or another. There were pictures of one hundred dollar bills spilling from half opened wallets. What a joke! My eyes wandered from one strolling pedestrian to the next. Already the early birds were showing signs of the private lives they led. There were teenage and twenty something young men and women in tight or ill-fitting clothes. Too tight or too short and in most cases worn too low to hide their bottoms draped in checkered underwear. The faces displayed the tell-tale signs of young lives spent on the streets and in clubs rather than in class rooms. Also present were small groups of men and women with cold hands clutching blue and green number slips. It was still another hour or so before 'post time' for the illegal street numbers and everyone who wanted to play still had ample time to get their numbers 'in' at the local bookie joint.

The one nearest "Ready Cash" paid Seven hundred dollars to one. This was two hundred dollars more than the State- run lottery paid for a one dollar bet and in most cases a hundred dollars more than other illegal joints elsewhere in the City. Needless to say they were taking all of the business in the area. People came from the Bronx and Brooklyn to partake in the bonanza even though it was as hard to hit a number as it was to hit a low flying airplane with a sling shot.

But just to be sure that their business stayed on top, the place held weekly raffles offering luxury items like televisions and laptops. They knew how to keep the players at their door even though one ran the risk of being swept up in a raid of the joint and going to jail. All regular players were given cartons of eggs each Saturday and of course, the occasional holiday chicken and turkey.

Seating was provided for those willing to wait for the first, second and third numbers as they 'came out 'an hour apart. The numbers were written on 3X5 inch cards and posted on a bulletin board like an announcement of changes to a bus or train schedule at a depot. It was a well-run operation and if you didn't 'hit' anything you could always leave full of coffee and donuts, albeit broke.

My eyes focused on a middle aged couple. They were tall. The woman wore sneakers but was clearly an inch or two taller than her male companion. They were walking arm in arm. Neither seemed to have a full set of teeth remaining. The jaws of both were drawn, as though they had just eaten half- ripened persimmons. Both had the unmistakable look of heroin or methadone addicts. It was a look I remembered from the 1960's and 70's. I watched them as they disappeared down the street, half expecting to see them stop at any moment and bow toward the pavement. Thinking these thoughts forced from me a smile and a moment of self -chastisement for my mean thoughts.

Suddenly, there was a thunderous crash. The sound of metal and fiberglass as two cars collided at the intersection. Moving from east to west a car had slammed into the rear fender of a gypsy cab and the ensuing damage was anything but minimal. No one had been injured but both drivers spilled out of their cars and into the street spewing fowl and venomous insults at one another. A sidewalk pedestrian who had witnessed the incident became embroiled in the controversy and was voicing his opinion as to which car he believed was to blame. His input was appreciated by one driver and rebuked by the other. The entire affair threatened to become a mini-riot if not for the intervention of a police van that seemed to have been cruising on the adjacent avenue. I looked up and spotted the bald pate of my friend as he crossed against the light on 7th Avenue and headed in my direction.

He was apologetic and I could have sworn he'd adopted a pretended limp in his walk as he approached me. But all was forgiven and he handed me the envelope containing my check which I gratefully took as I opened the door to Ready Cash. I stepped aside as a young woman pushing a baby stroller exited and took my place in the queue I was momentarily relieved that there were only five or six souls ahead of me but it turned out to be false gratification. I would remain in line for another twenty-five minutes as my friend paced the sidewalk peering into side windows to check my progress in line. He was annoyed that I seemed to be taking my time cashing the check. What nerve, I thought to myself! Eventually, I had my money and the lottery tickets I'd purchased. Carefully counting and stashing both away in my front pocket as I walked out the door and into the early afternoon sun.

The scene on the street was almost back to normal but I noted that the accident seemed to have attracted more clientele for Ready Cash. Nothing like a little excitement to bring people out like ants attracted to a slice of bread and I was at least glad that I had escaped the rush of those like me who for one reason or another would not or could not go to a local bank. Some of us were afraid that debt collectors would attach our accounts but most were receiving money from multiple State or Federal Agencies and didn't want to run the risk of being discovered. It was money they received for lying about babysitting when they didn't have a child in the world to sit for. Some agencies paid up to four hundred dollars a month for this sham. Another favorite was receiving money for illegally renting space in one's apartment while receiving S.S.I. or public assistance checks.

A next door neighbor was notorious for renting anything in her apartment that could be used to sleep on or in. Both couches in her small living room were occupied by two men (ex-cons) who were total strangers. Her extra bedroom was rented by a four hundred pound giant and his wife. She could charge extra for a couple. An attempt to charge him by the pound was rejected. Undaunted, she had even tried to rent half of her own bed to an older woman. Well, at least she hadn't yet rented the bath tub as I had heard was sometimes done. It was a riot and she was getting over like a fat rat and raking in an extra $320 each week on top of her SSI check and $200 in food stamps (the maximum allowance for one adult). She also wanted to get in on the faux babysitting scams going on all over the State.

I joined my friend and we headed for the nearest fast food joint for a bit of lunch. It would be a Popeye's Fried Chicken joint on the corner of Eighth Avenue. It wasn't exactly the healthiest way to begin the day but we were both hungry. I hadn't eaten a thing all morning and it was now past one in the afternoon. We entered and I strolled over to the next available window where I ordered a chicken biscuit, a coke and an apple cinnamon pie. I didn't notice what my friend ordered but I paid for everything and at the last minute I thanked the counter girl for her kindness. I thanked her in French since I noticed she'd just had a brief conversation with another customer in the language.

They had been talking about something personal and she looked at me like I was a talking pig. "You speak French," she demanded of me? "Why didn't you say so when you ordered your lunch?" "You did fine in English," I assured her. "You have no accent," I lied. The lie took her mind off the fact that she was embarrassed that she'd been overheard and she smiled as I turned away to join my friend. Already seated at a small table he had begun his lunch sans moi.

The eating tables and chairs at Popeye's are not made for

comfort. They are truly deserving of the name fast foods. Eat and get out. They are obviously someone's warped idea of a picnic table for munchkins with pot bellies and behinds constructed of steel. But at least the window seat was a plus and I settled in as best I could while making a futile attempt to catch up with my friend who was already halfway through his meal. I listened as he continued complaining about the long wait at the check cashing place. "I don't understand why it takes someone two hours to cash a check," he exaggerated. All they have to do is take the damn thing and push your chump change through the "f ...ing hole." But I was only half hearing him. My attention was riveted on the scene that was unfurling outside on the sidewalk. Several people had gathered to stare as a man walking his pit bull stood talking with someone.

There was nothing unusual about that except for the fact that he was gesticulating wildly and seemed to have completely forgotten that his pet, who was unleashed, was carrying a boom box radio in his mouth. It was firmly held in place by the animal's massive jaws.

The radio was tuned to a station and the dog never once let it fall to the ground. After about ten minutes, the man picked up a shopping bag he had placed on the ground nearby and continued down the street; the dog walked beside him still carrying the radio. The group of observers broke ranks still shaking the heads in wonderment and I continued eating and half listening to Mark's comments about the scene outside. He had witnessed it all once before he confessed.

But my mind had drifted to an uglier scene. It was a scene that had played out the night before in my brother's apartment where I was staying temporarily and where I had, I feared, worn out my welcome. It was nothing that I had done or said. Unless, one wanted to count that I had once again "forgotten" to take meat from the freezer to thaw in time for dinner. Why it was my responsibility to do so was still unclear. Especially since it was I who had bought the meat and fish to begin with and secondly, since he had a wife there who had forgotten the meaning of house work and the upkeep of her abode. Also, I hadn't been eating dinners with them for at least a week and I didn't feel up to being the chef for the fourth day in a row. The wife was a bad cook and whispered that she preferred my slightly European style of meals over his.

In any event, I had done my best to close the door to the room where I was paying rent. But it was no use. He'd been drinking again. He'd gotten his funds through direct deposit two days earlier and had been 'sippin' non-stop since then. Whenever this happened he would find something to say, place himself outside the door of my "room" and begin shouting his thoughts in a most obscene way. And this time had been one of the worst. Incidentally, I say my "room" not because it is but because it isn't in any sense of the word. I am paying for a small cot, four hangers in a wardrobe "there were five of them but the wife wanted to take one back. There is also floor space for my suitcase and a bag of dirty clothing. I can sit in his swivel chair. There is also a chest of drawers where I had been given two of the six. Actually, only one is usable for clothing as the other one is sectioned off into small compartments and when I was asked just the day before if there was an empty drawer available I nearly collapsed from the smell of her audacity.

As he ranted and raved I'd done everything in my power to keep from responding, as I knew it would only contribute to his tirade and I wanted, needed it to end so that I could get some sleep. Not too soon it all died down as he slept for about an hour. Again jolted from my reverie by the sound of his voice, as he shouted vulgarities at his wife - telling her to pack up and get out- threatening to leave himself or to do her bodily harm.

Then, pulling on his clothing, he was out the door and back yet another time to the store to buy more beer. He returned in twenty minutes or so and this time he turned the radio volume up loud enough to be heard three blocks away while announced that everyone in the house needed to "WAKE THE 'F' UP! I run a tight ship," he screamed at the top of his lungs! He theorized that everyone in the building played their music as loudly as they wanted and tonight he was going to do the same for as long as he pleased. This all began around 1:30 A.M. and I don't know when the music finally died. I was afraid to look at the clock.

By the time Mark called to say he was on his way uptown I'd had no sleep but here I sat, a few hours later tired and afraid to go back to the apartment. Not out of fear of safety but more out of pity for my brother.

He was in denial but it was clear: He needed help. When he was sober, he scarcely said more than a few words. Most times, when he was drinking the wife would place a hush finger over her lips and announce to me, "he's drinking again, but he'll be sober in the morning." Unfortunately, his sobriety was becoming more and more a rare event. He drank every day and some days were worse than others. Much worse.

And when he drank, to an observant person as I am, thank you for believing me, one could stand by and watch as his voice grew louder by the minute. The words growing more and more vulgar, the aggression, almost always against the wife, growing more and more vile, his demands more insistent and his comments to her about her family more and more debasing. But to himself, at these times he was the most intelligent, clever, thoughtful and kind person in the world, He knew everything about everything there was to know in the world or that had ever happened or was going to happen in the universe.

He needed no one's help, he had it all figured out and he could "hear a rat piss on cotton." He was also one of the most paranoid people I have ever met. "Don't be talking about me in my face!" You know me, I'll read a N..... What's the matter with you," he'd question his wife? At other times he would scarcely utter a sentence. This was witnessed by the times when his was sick from drink and curled up in his bed in a fetal position, staring at the TV in an otherwise darken room. During these brief sober times he wanted the doors double-locked and he'd tiptoe and peer through the peep hole as the neighbors came and went as though he was an agent for the KGB or the CIA. It was all disheartening to watch but he wanted and accepted help from no source. He was fine and just enjoying life in luxury and in his retirement.

Actually, the luxury about him could all be purchased and replaced for under ten grand and his retirement check was just shy of sixteen hundred a month. Some sweet life. But it was more than I had at the moment and that was my immediate problem. Oh, I had had more. Much more. But the last recession in the country had spoiled all of that and either I hadn't been frugal enough or it was meant to be because now I'd found myself in an unfortunate state of affairs to say the very least. But I have no regrets either. Life is meant to be enjoyed and I'd enjoyed mine in relative comfort and peace. You see I'm both unmarried and I've been celibate for the last decade and I intend to stay that way until there is a vaccine and a cure for A.I.D.S. Or, until I run into a virgin from some distant galaxy or black hole, no pun intended.

I suddenly remembered that I was sitting in Popeye's and in the few minutes that the previous night's events had replayed in my head I had completely tuned out everything else. I looked up at Mark apologetically as he called my name over and over. "Man, what planet were you visiting," he asked? "I'm sorry my friend," I said. "It was a rough night and you know what I'm talking about."

"I figured that when I saw you," he said in an understanding voice. I looked down at my tray of food. I had barely touched it and he asked me if I wanted the apple pie. "No." I said. "I have a taste for a slice of sweet potato pie but I don't know where to get it." "Oh,

I know a spot near here where they make good potato pies and it's in walking distance," he replied. "Where," I asked? I could tell he could sense my disbelief so I added. "Not everyone knows how to make really good sweet potato pie."

He seemed surprised by my answer and shrugged it off. "Sweet potato, meat potato, it's all the same stuff. What's the difference? It's all made with yams, isn't it?" "I can tell the difference and yams are yams. Sweet potatoes are just that," I offered in defense. But he wasn't listening. Seconds later we were on our way out of the door. But not before he noticed the group of young people who had taken seats behind me. Three young women and a young man. They were about 16 or 17 years old and all of them were wearing their jeans hanging half off their behinds as is the style. As usual the young man had gone a step farther than the girls and when he sat down his naked bottom was squarely on the wooded bench. We walked out the door. It had ceased to be either shocking or amusing. Older adults now found it just plain nasty we agreed and someone needed to put a stop to this nonsense or by summer half of the younger set might be walking the streets nude!

I made another effort to ask Mark what he knew about the pie place we were headed to. "I can really wait another day," I offered. "There's no need to go out of your way for this." "Why you don't let me handle it," he asked rather aggressively? It was almost a command and something in his voice reminded me of the night I'd just spent and I laughed out loud. "Why are you laughing?" He seemed almost annoyed. "Oh, I just thought of something private," I lied. I couldn't tell him the truth. I knew the truth but I couldn't yet put it into words.

At least not the words any sane person could understand. But I was getting there and his words were a big part of the conclusion I was beginning to draw. The same need to be abusive and overly aggressive on every point that was in any way critical for survival in the inner City. A don't tread on me attitude that was real or imagined. It was the same over-statement that served to push people further and further away instead of drawing them closer together. Yet, we were the first to say that our folks don't stick together like the other races. They never notice that we are part of the problem. It wasn't rocket science.

The Piranha effect I liked call it. My brother had stated it so many times. "This is my world," he'd shout. "And everything in it. I bought and paid for everything in here and nobody's gonna take it away from me. Not these no good Ns in Harlem or anyone else. The only person I have to be concerned about is you, my love." He'd scream these words as he turned to his live-in partner of seventeen or so years. "Do you understand that?" He'd demand her affirmative response! She would meekly give her yes answer, seconds before he lashed into her for the tenth time of the evening. Nothing and no one was sacred. Even her interest in watching the daily televangelist shows was criticized. Nothing it seemed was off-limits.

I ignored Mark's aggressive approach to a simple question as we continued walking toward the restaurant that he said served great pies. The day appeared to be moving at a feverish pitch. Kids, were out of schools and on their way home. An army of little ants with book bags strapped to their backs. The streets were crowded with groups of young and older men. Some had already spent half their checks and were now standing in animated conversations on stoops, in front of buildings and liquor stores, on corners and in front of barber shops. Some were engaged in dice games. It was an attempt to win what little money they could from someone less lucky or half high. And it wasn't difficult to tell which groups were high on marijuana and drugs and which were simply drunk from alcohol and beer consumption.

There were almost no females standing around idle and the few that could be seen appeared to be headed in a definite direction.

Even when they were walking two or more together there was a hint of purpose. Only the males of the species seemed to have a great deal of time to waste. They were a boisterous lot: talking loud and pretending to be involved in some great project as they eyed every female-young or old.

It was a point of habit and it was mostly peacocking. Many of the women were not attractive. I knew without listening that most of the conversation was about getting laid. It was almost routine even though someone would occasionally interject something that was either political or about sports.

As we passed I tried to avoid eye contact but I couldn't help that I was curious to see the faces and observe the copycat clothing of the players in this predictable screen play. Whether young or old they dressed alike: always in sneakers. Sneakers of the most expensive brand.

"Here we go. It's right next door to the beauty parlor," Mark announced. He seemed relieved to discover that the place was still open for business. "Oh," I lied. "I've passed this place several times." I didn't feel guilty for lying because I felt I had to say something to make up for my disappointment in seeing the seedy condition of the building. It was indeed next door to the beauty parlor. But it was barely next door and it gave the impression that a strong wind or an earthquake of a magnitude of one anywhere in the world would reduce it to the heap of rubble it was somehow avoiding by being glued to the sturdier buildings on either side of it. I tried not to be too judgmental. Sometimes surprises come in strange packages I silently reasoned.

Entering the place we took seats at the far end of the counter where I could see the comings and goings of the sidewalk traffic. At least what I could make out through the litany of paper signs placed on the window in haphazard fashion. These announced the menu specials. There were the usual burgers and fries, cakes and pies, fried chicken and beef liver with onions or spare ribs tips with collard greens. Another sign pronounced the business open 24 hours a day- 7 days a week. Free coffee was offered with the early morning staples of eggs with ham, bacon or sausages. Grits were extra as was oatmeal and cold cereal. They served margarine. One paid thirty cents for a pat of real butter.

I smiled back at the slightly overweight counter person and she made a comment about the jacket I was wearing. It was the second such comment of the day and I should have been used to it but I wasn't. Such compliments always left me embarrassed for having worn it. Actually, it was the only warm coat I had been able to salvage before I'd placed my things in storage months earlier. I had been wearing it on that day and had wanted to keep it on until my belongings arrived at the new place the following day. But that was all another story.

I was stuck with a reversible leather and dark mink jacket as my only winter coat. "Potato pie and coffee," I said to the smiling waitress. My friend said, "Make it two orders of pie but no coffee. I don't drink that stuff," he muttered this to no one in particular. She left to fill the order without bothering to wipe the countertop and I took a napkin and folded it to sop up the moisture that was still there. It had probably spilled when the last person ate lunch and I had been avoiding it like the plague. Images of Swine flu and Ebola and other dreaded infectious diseases floated through my head but I didn't want to embarrass her. I let it be.

She soon returned with both orders. Tasting the pie I turned away from her still smiling face in unashamed disappointment. "A man made this pie," I said wryly. I had meant it for the ears of my friend but the waitress overheard the comment and looked down at me as though she had been slapped in the face with a razor strap.

"How'd you know that," she asked. She was surprised? "Oh, I can always tell the difference between a man's sweet potato pie and one made by a woman," I said sheepishly." I was trying to cover my indiscretion with good humor but she was having none of it. "No, seriously. How did you know that my boss made that pie," she insisted?

"Well, I had no idea it was your boss who made the pie but like I told you, I can always tell the difference." "It smells cheesy," Mark interrupted. He was now laughing at our private joke and had fallen halfway off the stool in his amusement. "Tell, me what's the difference, so I'll know too because you sure as hell know what you're talking about," the waitress said loudly. She too was laughing. She whispered to her male counterpart what the joke was all about and then turned to me in sincerity.

"I'm sorry, I can't tell you because I don't know myself. It's just instinct I guess." I wasn't being truthful and I could tell she didn't believe me. She looked at me with a suspicious glance while I managed to eat a couple of spoons full. Finally giving up, I pushed it aside I took a big gulp from the glass of water. I was grateful that Mark had had the good sense to insist upon water being served with the pie.

I waited until Mark paid the bill. He hadn't eaten his either and he was laughing hysterically at the absurdity of the whole scene. Asking for another glass of water, I left the waitress a nice tip and drank hastily before we left laughing. The two of us spilled out onto the sidewalk like a couple of drunks, as the passersby's stared at us questioningly.

Things seemed to have heated up in the brief time we'd been in the restaurant. In New York City anything is possible and one never knows what is going to happen from one minute to the next.

As we approached the corner we realized that there was a fight in progress. Or, to be more accurate, one had already taken place. The damaged had already been done to the loser. From the looks of things a middle aged man was being restrained by two or three people. They were begging him not to re-enter a building. It was a building that I knew from past experience and it housed an illegal numbers spot on the first floor.

It was in a tiny two or three room apartment and after pushing the bell marked #2A patrons were allowed to enter. But whatever had happened there resulted in one man's front teeth being knocked from his mouth. He was bleeding profusely and as his companions tried to stop the flow of blood pouring from his mouth he seemed determined to return to exact his revenge on whomever was responsible for his present condition. His companions, seeing things a bit differently tried to stop him. Someone had given him a roll of paper towels to stem the flow of blood and they seemed to be convinced that returning to the scene would probably result in something else pouring from the man's head. Something white like his brains.

Whatever had happened to provoke the attack must have been the loser's fault because no one bothered to call 911 for an ambulance or the cops. It was a sickening scene and as we walked we circled the parked cars and crossed against the light. I mentioned to Mark that I was glad I hadn't bothered to eat the pie in the restaurant. This produced from him more laughter.

We stopped briefly in front of a pharmacy and smiled at the forty- something ex-prize fighter turned homeless crackhead who was shadow boxing and talking wildly to himself. Pedestrians whisked by looking at him disdainfully.

I'd promised to buy a large bottle of prune juice from the supermarket for my sister-in-law and I knew better than to return to the apartment without it. It was counted as a perk for her having the kindness to allow me to stay there for more than the rate she felt she could get for my room. There were a number of other perks that were expected of me. These included cleaning her house if my brother didn't feel up to it. She didn't do cleaning, she let everyone know. Also, part of the perks was a cooked meal for them a few times a week. She expected me to lend her of a few dollars every now and again. But she needed to be discreet about this because my brother disapproved. The money she borrowed was seldom paid back in full. It was "our" little secret.

She watched television in the privacy of her bedroom but when she was angry with me for daring to watch the evening news and not the same programs she watched she would use any excuse to try to annoy me. She'd call to me from her bedroom, "you left the light on in the kitchen." This was one of her favorites. Or, "someone is always calling here and hanging up. It must be for you, she would say accusingly."

"You never eat anything. There's no sense trying to watch your figure at your age," she'd taunt. The list of lies and accusations were endless and the foul language she used was as predictable as her protestations that 'people' were just trying to use her and take her kindness for weakness. She didn't think it right that she should have to answer the doorbell when visitors or the endless procession of loose cigarette buyers rang.

They didn't want anything except to purchase a few "loosies" from them. They were not operating a store and shouldn't have to accept pennies or the winning tickets from a two dollar scratch off lottery game as payment. She also should not have to make change for the black bastards in the fucking building. "I would say something nasty but I'm a Christian and I don't curse," she would moan. "But these mother f..s make me sick," she screamed sanctimoniously as she plodded from the front door with footsteps loud enough to challenge a Clydesdale.

Yes, she was a piece of work and as I went into the market to pick up the juice I scolded myself for not having the courage to just pack up and leave immediately. But I knew I'd be leaving at least a month prematurely. I bought the juice. Not that I expected it to shut her mouth. I knew that the symphony of confusion and chaos would continue for at least another two days. Maybe she'd drink the whole bottle of prune juice and then spend half her time running back and forth to the toilet while not noticing that I was present. I consoled my feelings with this malicious thought even though the thought made me feel guilty.

As I passed the cashier I glanced at the New York State poster containing the current list of daily midday and evening numbers. The Midday number was not anything I'd have chosen and I exited the store to take my leave of my friend. We stood near the dry cleaners chatting for few minutes more before parting ways. He was returning to a situation that was, although it shouldn't have been, a lot worse than my own and I didn't envy him. He was estranged from his wife and living with his son and daughter-in-law. They both smoked marijuana and left him with the baby sitting duties of a grandson only two weeks away from his terrible twos.

And I thought I had it bad! We made a half-hearted attempt to give one another courage, rehashing the sweet potato pie incident but it had lost most of its humor. Then, saying a hasty goodbye we walked in opposite directions. For me the pie had lost its reason to laugh in more ways than one. I didn't tell my friend what I was really thinking about its connection and significance to my experiences in life but I finally knew it in my head. I hurried to the house.

"Tony get yo' ass up off the floor. Comm'on now don't do that," she said. She moved toward him with her cell phone in hand. "You always do this."

It was only 6:30 P.M. But for the second time of the day I'd been forced to leave the apartment. Reluctantly, I'd found my way back down to one of the main hubs on the Hill. I didn't know any of these people except by sight. Although I had been inside this Dunkin' Donuts Coffee shop many times, I'd never done more than nod to them in respect as I placed my order and took a seat to join my friend Mark for a brief period of "kickin it "or to await his arrival while I patiently sipped my tea or hot chocolate.

It wasn't exactly the warmest place to be in winter but it sure beat the hell out of the local Chinese fast food spots on the Avenue. And it was becoming less a place of refuge for anyone with only a few dollars to spend and plenty of hours to kill. A sign had been posted limiting the time of table occupancy to 30 minutes and counter servers made regular rounds to make sure no one brought in food from an outside source. It wasn't a good indication that they had a great menu but I guess Management hadn't considered that aspect.

"Tony, I said get yo' yellow behind up off that floor!"

I didn't recall ever having seen Tony or the woman with the cell phone and I was surprised to discover they were not companions. "Oh," she said to whomever she was talking to on the phone, "I can't just leave him lying there on the ground. He's a Puerto Rican dude who lives in the neighborhood. I've been knowin' 'em for years." As she approached the spot where Tony struggled to get to his feet a man reached down and pulled him up, propping him against the soda and juice machine as though he was stacking a bevy of beverage cartons.

But Tony was unsteady on his feet and as he made his way past my chair near the rear of the café his legs became entangled and he fell to the floor again with a thud. "Oh shit man," the woman cried again. "You spen' more time on the ground than you do on your feet." And this time everyone laughed. But they ignored him as he pulled himself up and headed for the rest room. The woman took her seat about ten feet away from me and continued her telephone conversation. She attracted some attention when she mentioned that there was a young man standing outside the large plate glass window with his back to her. He was talking to a female friend and he seemed unaware that his pants were so low that most of his backside was showing as though he was a half-naked mannequin in a clothing store. I smiled to myself thinking that she hadn't noticed the log in her own eye. She had been putting on a similar display for me since I'd arrived some thirty minutes earlier.

It wasn't a great evening to be out for the weather was chilly and damp. It threatened to grow colder as the night wore on. Being outdoors was not my preference but I had few choices.

I had just wanted to get out of the house and away from the madness that was continuing non-stop. My brother was now almost as inebriated as the infamous Tony except that Tony appeared to be cut from a different cloth. He seemed innocuous and pathetic and certainly not threatening. As far as I was concerned this was a plus. I'd take a quiet drunk any day. I had tried to close the door of the room and concentrate on more pleasant things but it was no use.

My brother was obsessed with the fact that I had not eaten anything or prepared anything for them in a day or two. Never mind that I didn't want to eat or cook anything.

He didn't like cooking except on Sundays and he wasn't going to baby anyone. We were all adults. In fact, he didn't give a damn if nobody ate ever again in life. He had his and to hell with everybody else. Everybody else except his 'lovely' of course. Everybody could only have meant his brother since there were only three of us living there. Unable to take anymore punishment I'd left the house. Mumbling something about going to the pharmacy I headed for a quieter and a saner environment.

The moment I walked into the café and took a seat with my tea and biscuits in hand, I knew I had not bettered my immediate condition. There were two middle aged women seated at one of the only four tables in the place that were not facing the street. All the other seats were at counter tops and had the advantage of electrical outlets on their lone wall. Admittedly, it was great for laptop users and I'd almost brought mine along to do some work. The two women next to me were looking at a video on their machine, I saw no electrical cords. I sat there saying nothing but observing the comings and goings for about 20 minutes. It had been a long day and I really wanted to go back to my brother's place and relax but I knew that would be impossible.

"Excuse me, can I ask you a question," one of the ladies chirped?

I nodded my head in her direction and tried to avoid eye contact. I'd felt this coming but I was hopeful I could avoid another question about my jacket. "Well, I just wanted to know if you are interested in making extra money." That's a different approach I acknowledged to myself and I silently applauded her efforts. I looked at her in the eye. "Sure," I said. "I'm always interested in making money. What do you have in mind?" "Oh, if you have a few minutes you can look at his video and see for yourself," she said. "I have no interest in looking at a video and I'm not impressed by pictures. Why don't you explain to me exactly what you are talking about and then I'll tell you whether or not I'm interested," I answered. I was deliberately non-committal as I'd already made up my mind that she was peddling more than what was on the video.

After, a hesitant beginning she made a half-assed attempt to explain what she was selling. Finally, I interrupted her. I knew all along that it was a ruse and that she'd have done better to cut to the chase and say what was really on her mind. Even ask about my coat. "Well, I'll ask the Mrs. . . . . When I get home," I lied. "She makes most of the decisions in the family." It was another lie. About the fifth I'd found myself telling since early afternoon and the thought made me feel uncomfortable and almost ashamed but I felt I had no other choice. I had to stop the conversation permanently or I'd be in the middle of something I'd later regret. Apparently, it worked. "Let's go honey," the woman's companion announced. She stood and shut down the laptop. The lid snapped shut like the mouth of a giant clam as the two women gathered their belongings. In a minute they were both smiling and heading for the exit and I was relieved it had ended as it had. No one's feeling were hurt and no telephone numbers were needlessly exchanged. But the clock was ticking and I knew that I couldn't sit there lost in my thought and nursing my bruises for the rest of the night. I couldn't drink that much tea or hot chocolate and I hate latte or whatever that stuff is that they peddle to compete with Starbuck's.

I consoled myself with the knowledge that I would be rid of this entire situation in only a few weeks.

Thanks to the foresight and generosity of my lifelong friend I was being given a second chance to "muff things up" as she would have put it. She had passed away. She was gone just like so many other precious friendships in my life. And except for Mark and one or two others I was feeling almost alone in the City. But what to do? Where to go and how to start over? These were questions I needed to deal with in a sensible manner and I could afford no more mistakes. Not that I was unhappy with my accomplishments. I had done well.

Maybe the problem was that I'd outlived my resources and needed to find other outlets. Perhaps I'd just stayed too long at the fair, to borrow a cliché. It was one of the things I recalled about my now deceased benefactor. As a youngster during the great depression of the 1930's she'd known what it was like to live in difficult times. She was a decade older than I and she was always afraid of using up her savings on illness and inflation.

Luckily for me she hadn't and for that small bit I was immensely grateful to her.

It was time for a change in shifts at the café in more ways than one. Two or more of the counter people had dressed in street attire and were saying goodnight as they headed for the door. There was another change as two of the people I now recognized as local prostitutes strolled in and took their places near the front door. Also making an appearance were a couple of small time drug sellers. They always identified themselves because they immediately headed for the restroom to hide their wares. Well, I too needed to make my exit but for some unknown reason I hesitated. My mind returning once more to sweet potato pies. I was sure that I could now draw a bead on my feelings about them and here's the deal.

From what I have observed, sweet potato pies are a mirror image of life. Good, bad, up down. Not everyone can make one and you can always tell the difference between one made by a man and one that's made by a woman. Now I realize that this is a broad and dangerous route to travel. I am going to be criticized and berated by all those excellent professional bake chefs and amateur cooks who will swear that such and such makes the best sweet potato pies this side of the earth's hemisphere. And that is all true I am sure. I too have had foods prepared by males who are more than competent in their craft and I can but envy their skills.

But this is not just about sweet potato pies. This is about SWEET, potato pies. Pies that are made not only with skill but with TLC. It's not just about following the recipe. Anyone can do that. It's about the un-written ingredients that must be a part of a successful pie. Just enough of it, and the avoidance of over-indulgence and over-compensation. And therein lies the difference between the two species. I can tell the difference between the pies of a man and those made by a woman because men ALWAYS overdo things.

You can compare it to body language. It is like the extra swagger in the walk, the crossing of the ankles as the legs stretch out before the body in a busy restaurant or subway car. Almost taunting, almost inviting confrontation. The unspoken territorial game. This is my turf and I'll take my own sweet time in moving or deciding who can and cannot pass.

You can see it as both hands in the pocket as a male saunters down the street or the extra base in the voice to prove a point or to establish "one-up-man ship" when an argument turns ugly. In short, men always push things close to or over the edge. I know this because I too am a man. I used to do the same thing before I made a very conscious effort to pull back. Before I made the determination not to allow my emotions to overtake me. It's an easy thing to do but one has to first recognize it. Unfortunately, most of us are brought up learning how to first put our faces in it and then we spend a lifetime trying to do damage control. You can't overplay your hand and you can't make things too sweet after you've messed up. A pie that's been made too sweet is as bad as one without enough sugar. That's why you can always spot a pie that's been made by male hands. It may be lumpy. The color is always wrong. And the crust too pale, thick or flaky. Most of all the body of the pie is always too much. Overblown, it reflects our conventional theory: more is better.

Occasionally, it looks right from the outside. But a fork full will reveal a taste that is somewhere closer pumpkin. Sort of like someone who is pretending to be a good guy but is really a monster inside. There are a lot of us like that you know. Some of us abuse our girlfriends and wives and even our children. Calling them names like 'little n...s' and 'whores or bitches.

We deny them love and support when they need it most or until 'we feel' the urge.

And then, as one lady put it as she talked to someone on her cell phone, we expect them to say daddy this and daddy that at every twist and turn. Or, we'll dress for work and go to Church on Sunday's like everything's kosher. I know many will say "he's not talking about me or he's not speaking of the men I know." Well, if I'm not then I say the more power to you. And you and they are in a special place. I take my hat off. But I know differently. Denial is part of the problem and I am not saying that it can be totally fixed without stripping away what makes a man a man. Maybe it all can't be helped but some of the worse habits can be unlearned or at least understood. Just maybe that is good enough.

Yes, I can tell the difference between a man made sweet potato pie and one that is made by a woman but that is all. The rest are simply my observations and I need to make it crystal clear that am no scholar or sociologist. In fact, I don't even possess a university degree. But then you don't need a degree to see what I've observed in my years on planet Earth. Common sense will do just nicely thank you very much. And in case anyone is lacking in that department I have taken the liberty to include a recipe for making a really good sweet potato pie at the end of this treatise if anyone is interested.

I looked down at my laptop as I sat there on the side of the bed. It was 2:05 A.M. and the apartment was quiet. My brother and his wife had finally retired for the night and I was exhausted. I had spent the better part of the evening sitting in the Dunkin Donuts Café. Unable to take anymore tea into my system I got up from my seat and headed for the exit. I noted that the self-appointed doorman had returned to his usual position. He had a lot of courage because he'd been chased from the spot by the Oriental manager and two policemen only an hour or so earlier. They had warned him that he was facing arrest if he returned but as soon as the manager left for the evening he'd come back. I expected him to ask me for change as was his usual practice but he said nothing when he opened the door. I put a quarter in his hand and he smiled his thanks. Pulling my collar up around my ears to help ward off the cold night air I walked the dozen or so steps to the corner. "They got a lot of girls out here," the voice said. I looked up in the direction of the sound and into the face of the six foot -five or so black face.

But I said nothing as I stepped to the corner and walked with one or two other pedestrians. We hurried across the street in step with one another. Although against the light, we tried to avoid the menacing figure of the hulking street pimp. It was late and it had turned bitterly cold. But not cold enough to send scurrying for warmth the familiar faces in front of the liquor store. They'd been there since early afternoon: nine hours ago. It was enough time to have worked a full day. I walked quickly but reluctantly because I knew to expect more of the same that had driven me to the street more than a few hours earlier.

I was not disappointed. When I'd left the apartment things were moving toward an uncontrollable state. Apparently, they had reached a crescendo and they had spiraled completely off the charts. He was mad as a hatter. He screamed every word at the top of his lungs; as though we were two deaf mutes unable to hear the sound of a fire alarm. I went straight to the little spot known as my room. I didn't need this shit I told myself. I listened and waited for his ire to switch from my sister-in-law to me but it never came. He seemed to take no note that I was present and for that I was most grateful. Whatever had happened had wounded him to the quick and he didn't seem to be able to get past that point. Leaving the subject for five minutes, he'd return to it again and again or, each time he recalled her offense. He was livid.

I'd lived through moments like that with my mother threatening to give me a switching anytime she thought of some childish mischief I'd done. Back then it had all been just a threat and even as a young boy I'd had the good sense to keep my mouth shut. My sister-in-law was in the same unenviable position except that she kept apologizing for whatever "it" was every few minutes. The drama would cease for a few minutes and then begin anew again and again. This went on for the next two hours or until she begged to be left alone. But Mister was relentless. It was all too much and eventually the telephone began ringing every two minutes. He would answer the phone and scream into it that she was not at home and that the callers (her children and relatives) were to mind their own affairs. They were not to call anymore. Finally, he unplugged all of the phones in the apartment except the one in my room which for some unknown reason he told her to leave alone. It was the final straw. It was then that someone grew frightened enough to dial 911.

The police arrived at the door within minutes and made their presence felt.

The arrival of the cops only served to drive my brother further and further to the point of no return. But their arrival also gave the wife more courage. She began to over-act. If that was possible. She proclaimed she was afraid for her life. She even accused me, her brother-in-law of 'wanting 'to see her beaten to death. Of refusing to interfere when I knew that she was about to be bludgeoned to death. I was aghast! Bludgeoned to death with words, I asked myself? Even she admitted to the investigating officer that in 17 years of domesticity there had never been one single incident of physical violence between them. There was no doubt that when drinking he was verbally abusive and would pelt someone to death with the slings and arrows of outrageous curses. Maybe even with threats of violence thrown in for good measure. But the truth was that he wouldn't hit a lick at the proverbial "snake."

No, as severe as the disease was he wouldn't bust a grape. And I would bet my life on that. Moreover, I was aware that proper or not she could have walked out at any time without fear of retaliation. She knew it as well but this was about more than met the eye. Both had gone too far this time and now she wanted to win the game by making him feel that his reaction was worse than her original sin. Whatever that was. She wanted to go match point for match point. Even though the Academy Awards had already taken place for the year she wanted the Oscar: however posthumously. Charges and counter-charges continued until the two police officers, exhausted by the foolish and unnecessary waste of tax payers dollars left the bickering couple with the promise that if they had to return someone would be spending the night in the poky. There were only three of us in the apartment and I hadn't got involved in the madness. They certainly didn't mean my brother's wife. Taking the police officers at their word my brother dressed and walked out the door.

For more than an hour It was quiet and peaceful but soon the downstairs bell was ringing loudly an insistently. I was still trying to find out whose finger had been glued to it when there was loud banging on the door. When I opened it my brother half leaned, half fell into my arms. He was stinking drunk. But he wanted no help. Apparently, he'd visited a few local taverns and he had now lost all reason. But somehow he was still being very civil with me. This was his normal pattern and to his credit he never deviated from it. But he continued to insult his partner for her audacity in calling whomever it was she'd called and whomever in turn had called the cops. And he revisited her indiscretion yet another time.

From the vantage point of a short distance I pieced together their story. I learned that both parties had admitted to the police that their problem was of a 'sexual nature'. I was to discover the true nature of the problem. I listened with a shamed face as she repeated over and over that she was not a lesbian and that she had simply made a mistake. He had simply misread the tears or scratches on her body. He didn't believe her and I was beginning to believe that it might have been better to have admitted to an affair. Even to have invented such a story. He was irate. He was also emasculated and crushed. She should have understood this and kept her mouth shut but she didn't and things grew even uglier. Exhausted, I sat on the bed. Unable to sleep I turned out the lights and tried not to listen to what I'd rather have kept my ears from hearing but it was no use. I am sure I counted every hour their 8-day chime clock struck between 11 P.M. and 4 A.M. Until finally, tired beyond reason, I lay fully clothed upon the narrow bed. I closed my eyes until I fell into a deep sleep.

Somewhere between 4 a.m. and daybreak my sister-in-law left the house in her robe and slippers. She hailed a taxi and fled to the apartment of one of her daughters. Eliza had made it safely across the icy river waters ahead of the blood hounds. About 9 a.m. my brother knocked on my door and announced that he too was making his exit: stage left. He was going to Empire City he said. There he would gamble away the rent money or at least half of it to calm his nerves. To assuage his frustrations he'd drown them in drink and vice. The drama was continuing. The plot thickening. I was tired of the childish games and the bullshit. But what could I do? I was stuck in the middle of the nonsense and at least one month shy of being able to put it all behind me.

It was only after I stumbled from my bed and showered that I was able to pull my thoughts together and prepare for what would turn out to be incredibly, an even more chaotic day than the day before. It wasn't check day again but it was just as bad. Those who still had money left were still spending it in frivolous fashion. And a few of those who didn't would now sell their food stamps to the local bodegas and mini-markets at a ratio of 2-1. That is: in return for every two dollars of food stamps, 'the man' would pay one paper dollar. The number playing, liquor buying, cigarettes, sex and drugs could therefore be subsidized for yet another day.

It was the full of morning and as I left the apartment and walked out for a newspaper and a cup of tea I was met by the baleful eyes of the gossips who lived in the building and in the two adjacent complexes. I didn't blame them since undoubtedly they had been kept awake listening to the drama through the paper-thin walls of the apartments. There were questions in their stares but they knew better than to ask them of me as I walked by tipping my hat to them as was my practice. Regardless of ethnicity it was a gesture that always made people ill at ease. It was polite but standoffish. I knew they were unaccustomed to it and it forced from them a respect that they would not otherwise have given to most living in the area.

The day was a glorious one and with the newspaper I settled on a park bench and lost myself in thought, half nodding in a fitful slumber. I awoke a quarter hour or so later to the sound of police sirens. I'd learned early that in this neighborhood it was always an ominous sign but I was relieved to discover I'd slept through the gun shots. Asking questions I was told there had been some sort of disturbance in the next block and four or five shots had been fired. When the shooting ceased and people returned to their previous positions from behind parked cars it was discovered that one resident would not be going anywhere. He had been shot through the skull and lay on the ground as dead as cabbage leaves. Whether he had been shot by accident or design was unclear. I decided not to satisfy my curiosity with the answer.

My friend Mark had arrived and as we sat talking I saw my brother walking toward the building. He had a grocery bag in his hand and seemed in good spirits. We were close to the corner of the street and we'd been sitting there for an hour or more. We were rehashing the events of the previous twenty-four hours and laughing our heads off at the absurdity of it all. I am sure my brother thought he would come home early and try to make amends for the previous day. A kind of kiss and make up with the wife. You know what I mean! If these were his intentions he was to be sorely disappointed. Oh, the wife had returned home. But she had come home with a half dozen family members and they were hell-bent on having it out with him. Ganging up on him and whoever was supporting him. Someone like yours truly. I said a quick goodbye to Mark and moved toward the house in a dash. By the time I put my key in the door the festivities were in full swing. The accusations and threats, the admonitions and curses. And for yet another day: the cops. Some thoughtful neighbor had heard it all and called them. We arrived simultaneously. I, the law and a customer who wanted to purchase two of the illegally sold cigarettes: the loosies. I quickly got rid of the client, closed the door and walked into the apartment. It was, as they say, a good thing.

If the dear wife had intended to stir up a hornet's nest she had done so beyond her wildest anticipations. In fact, she couldn't have done any better had she been seated at a draft table with a ruler. In reality, she'd only meant to draw attention to her husband's increasing problem with drink but things had spiraled out of control and now, with all her strength Pandora couldn't reseal the box. The police officers came ready to put handcuffs on my brother, though they were not exactly sure what he'd done wrong. They also wanted to clear her family from the apartment but decided better of it when they realized that without their presence they could not coax a reluctant wife to give testimony against her suddenly remorseful and contrite spouse. The family, which had demanded my instant and permanent removal from the apartment were told unceremoniously that it was unlawful to even try since I'd done nothing untoward and had lived there for more than thirty days. My brother immediately ingratiated himself and atoned for all his past sins toward me by declaring that if I left he too would be right behind me.

The wife was devastated by these revelations and everyone had to develop a kinder and gentler tone toward me. Save one young woman, a stripper by profession and granddaughter of the wife who wanted my head. She declared to all that if my brother ever touched her grandmother I was a dead man. A dead man walking. I brushed aside the impudence of the young heifer; not taking the threat seriously. With police officers still in the apartment she never understood the folly of her statement. She never understood that grandmother wasn't exactly an innocent lamb in all of this. I'd heard her sharp and ugly tongue more than once.

At last things calmed down and everyone fled the apartment. But not before one of the officers called me aside and placed a machete in my hands. It had been found in a closet and the wife told everyone that my brother had shaken it in her face the night before. It was an illegal weapon in the State of New York and by law my brother could have been arrested for having it in his possession. But the cop did a curious thing. He instructed me to get rid of it. "Get this thing out of here and don't come back with it," he said. "We'll return in exactly two hours and if it is still here your brother is going to jail." I got rid of it as told but the cops never came back to the apartment. It wasn't the first time a law enforcement officer had looked the other way in my presence and I was grateful but perplexed. I suppose it is my hair style, although I haven't got very much of that left on my head anymore.

And now, with the events of the last couple of days still hovering over his head like a battalion of angry wasps, my brother continued to get drunk. He also decided that he would prepare the evening meal. He'd fry chicken and mash potatoes. He would throw in a side of asparagus tips and biscuits and for dessert there'd be ice cream. Oh yeah, remember the bag I saw him with earlier? It contained ingredients for making a pie. In an effort to make up to the Missus he had decided to appeal to her stomach and her insatiable appetite for sweets. He'd bake a sweet potato pie. She loved them so he'd bought two pie shells of the Mrs. Smith's variety. "They're tasty," he boasted as though he was the poster boy for the Smith Company.

Well, the pies would have to wait, pie shells and all because he would fall asleep on the couch. I cooked the meal and let him snore knowing that when he awoke he would begin his third night of terror. But it would be his last until the coming weekend. After all, he still had money left from his check. I knew that there was nothing I could do to prevent this. I certainly wasn't going to try to stop him from drinking and I would never attempt to bake a sweet potato pie. For my money men can't make sweet potato pies. Not even me.

THE END

March 14th, 2010

Man Made Sweet Potato Pie

Four large sweet potatoes boiled in their skins. Cool. When done this way the skin slips off easily using just the fingers. And please note that yams are not sweet potatoes. They are both tubers but they are otherwise unrelated. If your store only has yams you are already beginning at a disadvantage but go ahead and take your best shot. Just remember that it is now a yam pie. Also, I said four, not five- large potatoes. Not huge ones. There is a difference. Please gentlemen, size matters but bigger is not better!

You will also need two cups of white refined sugar. The old fashioned kind. Not sweeteners or substitutes like high fructose corn syrup or the easy- pour very fine sugars now on the market.

I also like to add about one half cup of dark brown sugar. Not too much. It is as much for color as it is for taste.

One stick of butter. Butter that is and not margarine or its substitutes. It doesn't make a difference if it is Salted or not but if you can get the unsalted kind then do so. It's your call. You da man, bro.

About one half teaspoon of cinnamon and one half teaspoon of nutmeg. I say measure it because we all have different size fingers and you will never figure out what a pinch is if I turn you lose too soon. And you know what I'm talking about. You can also add a half teaspoon of cornstarch just to make sure it holds together but don't overdo it. Half teaspoon and that is all or add a well-beaten egg.

Finally, you can use one half cup of milk or to make it a bit creamier you can substitute half and half. Also sweetened condensed milk is excellent but only one half cup.

Now Sir, this does not mean that I have given you license to go for broke. No, heavy cream, yogurt or Cream cheese in place of the half and half or in addition to it just for taste or to add your own touch.

This is plain sweet potato pie and not your own invention that you'll be sorry in twenty years you didn't file a patent for. Don't worry. Some enterprising bloke is not going to make a mint off "your" idea while you sit struggling in your retirement just to keep a roof over your head. Okay?

You are not going to need anything else except a good store bought pie shell. And there are a few around that you can use. Or if you follow directions you can use the prepared dough bought in your local super market, or even make it from scratch although this is another story and I wouldn't recommend it to a novice.

And now that we understand one another here is all you do.

In a large bowl mash the peeled potatoes until they are reasonably smooth. Use a simple hand masher. That will do just fine. Don't blend or dump the whole thing in a newfangled electric mixer. You're not ready for that step. Not yet anyway and besides, it's not necessary to do for one or two pies. Just make sure that there are no lumps or strings. If there are, take them out. That is why I sometimes add an extra potato. You know. Just in case I come up short. Yeah, you get it!

From this point, it doesn't matter what you do to it. Even you can't muff things up. Just add the other ingredients one at a time and mix them all together. Obviously, the butter must be melted in advance in a small pan. But please, over low heat. Don't burn the butter, sir.

Having put everything together. Not churned or mixed to death, pour the mixture into the pie shell that you have placed ON AN UNGREASED BAKING PAN and put the thing in an oven preheated to about 375 degrees F. Not a toaster oven or a microwave to speed things up for goodness sake. Just your garden variety oven. You can find the oven easily enough. It is underneath the burners where you prepare your franks and beans or your earth-shattering barbequed eggs.

And this is most important. Leave at least one quarter inch of space at the top of the shell. Don't fill it all the way to the top and then smooth it over with a spatula. This is a sweet potato pie, not a deep dish apple pie or a chicken pot pie. Know when to stop, Sir!

Cook it for about 35-40 minutes and take it out to cool. Don't try to eat it hot. It will burn. It will also fall apart and you will have a kind of spoon pudding. You'll have that anyway after you have spooned a quart ice cream onto the top and then washed it down with beer.

If you've taken your time and not forgotten anything or left it in the oven for too long (use a timer and not the clock on the TV) it should come out reasonably tasty.

No, it won't be as good as the pies made by the other sex but what is?

You gave it your best shot and if the TLC is missing no one can blame you.

My man!

TIME GROWS

TIME GROWS JUST a little. It's almost indiscreet. Ounce by ounce and inch by inch, like freshly poured concrete.

A day none other can surpass. And then another fading fast that leaves me nearly breathless. That leaves me not quite right.

Still Time grows quick. Impatient time, unbridled and improved. A touch of grey, a wisp of salt a heart that can be moved.

I smile when feelings stir the loins- a glimpse of what was once. Does time still thrive beneath the snow that lie atop it all?

Nay, just a brief reminder still that time is passing me. That hour by hour, that day by day. That what must be must be.

Ce qui sera, sera!

July 09, 2019
13:19

Le temps de Dieu n'est pas cela des humains!

Printed in the United States
By Bookmasters